# *Seven Stories*

D0869069

# Gina Berriault

COUNTERPOINT

Berkeley, California

COUNTERPOINTS 8

SEVEN STORIES

Library of Congress Cataloging-in-Publication Data
Names: Berriault, Gina, author.
Title: Seven stories / Gina Berriault.
Description: First Counterpoint edition. | Berkeley, California :
    Counterpoint, 2022. | Series: Counterpoints ; 8
Identifiers: LCCN 2021054744 | ISBN 9781640095458
    (paperback) | ISBN 9781640095465 (ebook)
Subjects: LCGFT: Short stories.
Classification: LCC PS3552.E738 S48 2022 | DDC
    813/.54—dc23/eng20211110
LC record available at https://lccn.loc.gov/2021054744

*Series cover designed by Jenny Carrow*
*Cover designed by Lexi Earle*
*Series interior designed by Jordan Koluch*
*Book designed by Laura Berry*

COUNTERPOINT
2560 Ninth Street, Suite 318
Berkeley, CA 94710
www.counterpointpress.com

Printed in the United States of America

10  9  8  7  6  5  4  3  2  1

# Contents

# SEVEN
# STORIES

# THE INFINITE
# PASSION OF
# EXPECTATION

The girl and the elderly man descended the steep stairs to the channel's narrow beach and walked along by the water's edge. Several small fishing boats were moving out to sea, passing a freighter entering the bay, booms raised, a foreign name at her bow. His sturdy hiking boots came down flatly on the firm sand, the same way they came down on the trails of the mountain that he climbed, staff in hand, every Sunday. Up in his elegant neighborhood, on the cliff above the channel, he stamped along the side-walks in the same way, his long, stiff legs attempting ease and flair. He appeared to feel no differences in terrain. The day was cold, and every time the little transparent fans of water swept in and drew back, the wet sand mirrored a clear sky and the sun on its way down. He wore an overcoat, a cap, and a thick muffler, and, with his head high, his large, arched nose set into the currents of air from off the ocean, he described for her his fantasy of their honeymoon in Mexico.

He was jovial, he laughed his English laugh that was like a bird's hooting, like a very sincere imitation of a laugh. If she married him, he said, she, so many years younger, could take a young lover and he would not protest. The psychologist was seventy-nine, but he allowed himself great expectations of love and other pleasures, and advised her to do the same. She always mocked herself for dreams, because to dream was to delude herself. She was a waitress and lived in a neighborhood of littered streets, where rusting cars stood unmoved for months. She brought him ten dollars each visit, sometimes more, sometimes less; he asked of her only a fee she could afford. Since she always looked downward in her own surroundings, avoiding the scene that might be all there was to her future, she could not look upward in his surroundings, resisting its dazzling diminishment of her. But out on these walks with him she tried looking up. It was what she had come to see him for—that he might reveal to her how to look up and around.

On their other walks and now, he told her about his life. She had only to ask, and he was off into memory, and memory took on a prophetic sound. His life seemed like a life expected and not yet lived, and it sounded that way because, within the over-coat, was a youth, someone always look-ing forward. The girl wondered if he were outstripping time, with his long stride and emphatic soles, and if his expectation of love and other pleasures served the same purpose. He was born in Pontefract, in England, a Roman name, meaning broken bridge. He had been a sick child, suffering from rheumatic fever. In his twenties he was a rector, and he and his first wife, emanci-pated from their time, each had a lover, and some very modern nights went on in the rectory. They traveled to Vienna to see what psychoanalysis was all about. Freud was ill and referred them to Rank, and as soon as introductions were over, his wife and Rank were lovers. "She divorced me," he said, "and had a child by that fellow. But since he wasn't the marrying kind, I gave his son my family name, and they came with me to

America. She hallucinates her Otto," he told her. "Otto guides her to wise decisions."

The wife of his youth lived in a small town across the bay, and he often went over to work in her garden. Once, the girl passed her on the path, and the woman, going hastily to her car, stepped shyly aside like a country schoolteacher afraid of a student; and the girl, too, stepped sideways shyly, knowing, without ever having seen her, who she was, even though the woman—tall, broad-hipped, freckled, a gray braid fuzzed with amber wound around her head—failed to answer the description in the girl's imagination. Some days after, the girl encountered her again, in a dream, as she was years ago: a very slender young woman in a long white skirt, her amber hair to her waist, her eyes coal black with ardor.

On the way home through his neighborhood, he took her hand and tucked it into the crook of his arm, and this gesture, by drawing her up against him, hindered her step and his and slowed them down. His house was Spanish style, common to that seaward section of San Francisco. Inside, everything was heavily antique—carven furniture and cloisonné vases and thin and dusty Oriental carpets. With him lived the family that was to inherit his estate—friends who had moved in with him when his second wife died; but the atmosphere the family provided seemed, to the girl, a turnabout one, as if he were an adventurous uncle, long away and now come home to them at last, cheerily grateful, bearing a fortune. He had no children, he had no brother, and his only sister, older than he and unmarried, lived in a village in England and was in no need of an inheritance. For several months after the family moved in, the husband, who was an organist at the Episcopal church, gave piano lessons at home, and the innocent banality of repeated notes sounded from a far room while the psychologist sat in the study with his clients. A month ago the husband left, and everything grew quiet. Occasionally, the son was seen about the house—a high school track star, small and blond like his mother, impassive like his father, his legs usually bare.

The psychologist took off his overcoat and cap, left on his muffler, and went into his study. The girl was offered tea by the woman, and they sat down in a tête-à-tête position at a corner of the table. Now that the girl was a companion on his walks, the woman expected a womanly intimacy with her. They were going away for a week, she and her son, and would the girl please stay with the old man and take care of him? He couldn't even boil an egg or make a pot of tea, and two months ago he'd had a spell, he had fainted as he was climbing the stairs to bed. They were going to visit her sister in Kansas. She had composed a song about the loss of her husband's love, and she was taking the song to her sister. Her sister, she said, had a beautiful voice.

The sun over the woman's shoulder was like an accomplice's face, striking down the girl's resistance. And she heard herself confiding—"He asked me to marry him"— knowing that she would not and knowing why she had told the woman. Because to speculate about the possibility was to accept his esteem of her. At times it was necessary to grant the name of love to something less than love.

On the day the woman and her son left, the girl came half an hour before their departure. The woman, already wearing a coat and hat, led the way upstairs and opened, first, the door to the psychologist's bedroom. It seemed a trespass, entering that very small room, its space taken up by a mirrorless bureau and a bed of bird's-eye maple that appeared higher than most and was covered by a faded red quilt. On the bureau was a doily, a tin box of watercolors, a nautilus shell, and a shallow drawer from a cabinet, in which lay, under glass, several tiny bird's eggs of delicate tints. And pinned to the wallpaper were pages cut from magazines of another decade—the faces of young and wholesome beauties, girls with short, marcelled hair, cherry-red lips, plump cheeks, and little white collars. She had expected the faces of the mentors of his spirit, of Thoreau, of Gandhi, of the other great men whose words he quoted for her like passwords into the realm of wisdom.

The woman led the way across the hall and into the master bedroom. It was the woman's room and would be the girl's. A large, almost empty room, with a double bed no longer shared by her husband, a spindly dresser, a fireplace never used. It was as if a servant, or someone awaiting a more prosperous time, had moved into a room whose call for elegance she could not yet answer. The woman stood with her back to the narrow glass doors that led onto a balcony, her eyes the same cold blue of the winter sky in the row of panes.

"This house is ours," the woman said. "What's his is ours."

There was a cringe in the woman's body, so slight a cringe it would have gone unnoticed by the girl, but the open coat seemed hung upon a sudden emptiness. The girl was being told that the old man's fantasies were shaking the foundation of the house, of the son's future, and of the woman's own fantasies of an affluent old age. It was an accusation, and she chose not to answer it and not to ease the woman's fears. If she were to assure the woman that her desires had no bearing on anyone living in that house, her denial would seem untrue and go unheard, because the woman saw her now as the man saw her, a figure fortified by her youth and by her appeal and by her future, a time when all that she would want of life might come about.

Alone, she set her suitcase on a chair, refusing the drawer the woman had emptied and left open. The woman and her son were gone, after a flurry of banging doors and good-byes. Faintly, up through the floor, came the murmur of the two men in the study. A burst of emotion—the client's voice raised in anger or anguish and the psychologist's voice rising in order to calm. Silence again, the silence of the substantiality of the house and of the triumph of reason.

"We're both so thin," he said when he

embraced her and they were alone, by the table set for supper. The remark was a jocular hint of intimacy to come. He poured a sweet blackberry wine, and was sipping the last of his second glass when she began to sip her first glass. "She offered herself to me," he said. "She came into my room not long after her husband left her. She had only her kimono on and it was open to her navel. She said she just wanted to say good night, but I knew what was on her mind. But she doesn't attract me. No." How lightly he told it. She felt shame, hearing about the woman's secret dismissal.

After supper he went into his study with a client, and she left a note on the table, telling him she had gone to pick up something she had forgotten to bring. Roaming out into the night to avoid as long as possible the confrontation with the unknown person within his familiar person, she rode a streetcar that went toward the ocean and, at the end of the line, remained in her seat while the motorman drank coffee from a thermos and read a newspaper. From over the sand dunes came the sound of heavy breakers. She gazed out into the dark, avoiding the reflection of her face in the glass, but after a time she turned toward it, because, half-dark and obscure, her face seemed to be enticing into itself a future of love and wisdom, like a future beauty.

By the time she returned to his neighborhood the lights were out in most of the houses. The leaves of the birch in his yard shone like gold in the light from his living room window; either he had left the lamps on for her and was upstairs, asleep, or he was in the living room, waiting for the turn of her key. He was lying on the sofa.

He sat up, very erect, curving his long, bony, graceful hands one upon the other on his crossed knees. "Now I know you," he said. "You are cold. You may never be able to love anyone and so you will never be loved."

In terror, trembling, she sat down in a chair distant from him. She believed that he had perceived a fatal flaw, at last. The present moment seemed a lifetime later, and all that she had wanted of herself, of life, had never come about, because of that fatal flaw.

"You can change, however," he said. "There's time enough to change. That's why I prefer to work with the young."

She went up the stairs and into her room, closing the door. She sat on the bed, unable to stop the trembling that became even more severe in the large, humble bedroom, unable to believe that he would resort to trickery, this man who had spent so many years revealing to others the trickery of their minds. She heard him in the hallway and in his room, fussing sounds, discordant with his familiar presence. He knocked, waited a moment, and opened the door.

He had removed his shirt, and the lamp shone on the smooth flesh of his long chest, on flesh made slack by the downward pull of age. He stood in the doorway, silent, awkward, as if preoccupied with more important matters than this muddled seduction.

"We ought at least to say good night," he said, and when she complied he remained where he was, and she knew that he wanted her to glance up again at his naked chest to see how young it appeared and how yearning. "My door remains open," he said, and left hers open.

She closed the door, undressed, and lay down, and in the dark the call within herself to respond to him flared up. She imagined herself leaving her bed and lying down beside him. But, lying alone, observing through the narrow panes the clusters of lights atop the dark mountains across the channel, she knew that the longing was not for him but for a life of love and wisdom. There was another way to prove that she was a loving woman, that there was no fatal flaw, and the other way was to give herself over to expectation, as to a passion.

RISING EARLY, SHE found a note under her door. His handwriting was of many peaks, the aspiring style of a century ago. He likened her behavior to that of his first wife, way back before they were married, when she had tantalized him so frequently and always fled. It was a humorous, forgiving note, changing her into that other girl of sixty years ago. The weather was fair, he wrote, and he was off by early bus to his mountain across the bay, there to climb his trails, staff in hand and knapsack on his back. *And I still love you.*

That evening he was jovial again. He drank his blackberry wine at supper; sat with her on the sofa and read aloud from his collected essays, *Religion and Science in the Light of Psychoanalysis*, often closing the small, red leather book to repudiate the theories of his youth; gave her, as gifts, Kierkegaard's *Purity of Heart* and three novels of Conrad in leather bindings; and appeared again, briefly, at her door, his chest bare.

She went out again, a few nights later, to visit a friend, and he escorted her graciously to the door. "Come back any time you need to see me," he called after her. Puzzled, she turned on the path. The light from within the house shone around his dark figure in the rectangle of the open door. "But I live here for now," she called back, flapping her coat out on both sides to make herself more evident to him. "Of course! Of course! I forgot!" he laughed, stamping his foot, dismayed with himself. And she knew that her presence was not so intense a presence as they thought. It would not matter to him as the days went by, as the years left to him went by, that she had not come into his bed.

On the last night, before they went upstairs and after switching off the lamps, he stood at a distance from her, gazing down. "I am senile now, I think," he said. "I see signs of it. Landslides go on in there." The declaration in the dark, the shifting feet, the gazing down, all were disclosures of his fear that she might, on this last night, come to him at last.

The girl left the house early, before the woman and her son appeared. She looked for him through the house and found him at a window downstairs, almost obscured at first sight by the swath of morning light in which he stood. With shaving brush in hand and a white linen hand towel around his neck, he was watching a flock of birds in branches close to the pane, birds so tiny she mistook them for fluttering leaves. He told her their name, speaking in a whisper toward the birds, his profile entranced as if by his whole life.

The girl never entered the house again, and she did not see him for a year. In that year she got along by remembering his words of wisdom, lifting her head again and again above deep waters to hear his voice. When she could not hear him anymore, she phoned him and they arranged to meet on the beach below his house. The only difference she could see, watching him from below, was that he descended the long stairs with more care, as if time were now underfoot. Other than that, he seemed the same. But as they talked, seated side by side on a rock, she saw that he had drawn back unto himself his life's expectations. They were way inside, and they required, now, no other person for their fulfillment.

# THE TEA CEREMONY

Ocean liners sailed right on through the Depression years, and certain persons who had jobs, like teachers, could go and visit countries that were not at war. Miss Furguson had been to Japan. She brought to school a silk kimono purchased in Nagasaki, for a sum she would not divulge. One of the boys asked her outright, but she bowed her head, smiling tolerantly. It's not polite to ask those kinds of questions, she said, so we don't answer them. The boy, humiliated, angry, turned his whole body sideways in his seat and stared out the window.

The kimono hung on a long bamboo rod with a black silk tassel at each end, showing off the wide sleeves to advantage and the hand-painted scene of a teahouse and white cranes wading in a stream. It had a red silk lining. You could file along before it but you could not touch it. Miss Furguson fingered the silk between her thumb and forefinger. The feel of silk, nothing like it, she said.

Only for Jolie Lotta, as she filed by, did Miss Furguson point out the kimono's many precious details. What a beautiful girl she was, Jolie Lotta. How pale and clear her skin, how long and light her hair, how modestly plump her hands, ready for those gold rings promising bliss, her bare legs ready for skin-pale silk stockings, her complete person like a presentation of a virtue for all to see. A girl held in such high esteem by Miss Furguson, the boys kept their distance. And how could it be that Jolie Lotta was best friends with me?

Tall dry weeds and wild oats—that was the outskirts of the town and its empty lots, but you'd be surprised by who you'd find in the drugstore. Jolie Lotta's mother was the most beautiful woman I had ever seen in all my thirteen years of learning what beauty is. Hers was beyond comparison with the pretty ones in our class, already preening themselves for their entry into the market-place. She wore a clerk's tan uniform, her hair, a darker blonde than her daughter's, was coiled at the nape of her neck, and her large, hazel eyes held a certainty of her own beauty, a lovely basking, a look that I hoped I might show for myself someday and knew I never could.

My mother, said Jolie Lotta to me one day, wants me to stop being friends with you. She named three girls who went around together and with nobody else, one whose father was the mayor, one whose father was the city attorney, and one whose father was simply rich, and it was these three girls whom her mother wanted for her friends. I already knew what was unfavorable about me, but I knew more emphatically then. I became who I was in her mother's beautiful eyes. Beauty can do that to you. I became the girl who Jolie Lotta's mother saw, those few minutes in the drugstore when she appeared to be seeing only her daughter. How skinny my legs, how scrawny my hands, still an agile child's hands, sun-browned, stained with colored inks, and how unruly my dark hair, and how crazily stitched my clothes by my mother going blind and insisting on sewing up the tears. With the prescience some children have of their life to come, I knew then that I would keep my own distance from them, from those who were perfected by their beauty and by everybody's adoration. The farther the distance, the less the longing to be like them.

Miss Furguson asked the class to point to the one among us who we liked the best. I pointed to the girl who was a better artist than myself, and found their fingers pointing at me. A mistake! I was entangled hand and foot in Miss Furguson's mistaken question. They would not have chosen me had they known everything about me, the shameful things that only I knew. Oh, is it Delia? said Miss Furguson, not looking at me, looking around to see if some fingers were pointing at some others, and found that they were. Ah hah, this country is a democracy, she said, and smiled at me consolingly.

Noontime, I began to go around alone, seeking places from where I could not see the promenading girls, all perfecting themselves. Then the shyest girl in class, who was never heard from, began to follow me around. She spoke not one word, that Wilma, her large, darkly shining eyes doing all the pleading of me to be her best friend. Go away, I said. Go away and stay away. She would not go, she would not let me be alone. Until one day I pounded on her back, and then she went away. And even as I had thought I was the boy who asked Miss Furguson the price of her kimono, I thought I was that girl, that Wilma. I did not want to be them. It was no place for me to be, there in their wounded hearts, but there I was.

One morning, the moment the bell rang, we went quickly into the classroom, wanting to impress Miss Furguson with our eagerness to obey rules. Jolie Lotta's mother was in the headlines of the town newspaper, caught at doing something disastrously wrong, something against the strictest of all rules. Adrianna Lotta, a divorced woman, living with her mother and thirteen-year-old daughter, Jolie, in the Maple Apartments on Bee Street, was found near death at the side of her lover, City Councilman Mack McPorter, a married man, in the Seaside Motel. Asphyxiated by a leaking gas heater, they were both rescued from death in the nick of time. Our eyes alight, we sat down at our desks. Jolie Lotta was absent.

Miss Furguson, of course, knew more than we knew about this event. It was expected of teachers to know more about any event. She said nothing, but what she knew about this one filled out her person, elevating her short stature, swelling her bosom, enriching her voice, giving us a more complete picture of her than we'd ever had, and that usual stance of hers when she faced us, legs close together, feet close together, became curiously noticeable. Entranced, we watched her every move.

Some persons are made more perfect by what befalls them, as if whatever befalls them can never make them less, can never bring them low, as it might others. I figured this out in the five days Jolie Lotta was absent. I'd glance up at Miss Furguson engrossed at her desk and suspect her of perfecting Jolie Lotta ever more. One morning she was with us again, slipping in, paler, less spirited. The girls who had taken her into their circle enclosed her again, a prize.

Not many days after Jolie Lotta's return, Miss Furguson showed us the Japanese tea ceremony. Set before us were two round black cushions with a shimmer to them, so they must be silk, and a low, lacquered table. On the table was a pale green teapot, so precious you felt undeserving of the sight of it, and two little pale green bowls. While we were out at afternoon recess, Miss Furguson had set things up, to surprise us. On her desk was a bouquet of little yellow flowers in a vase. It had not been there before.

She stood before us, facing us, happier than we had ever seen her. The tea ceremony, she said, is perfectly beautiful, as you will see. If Miss Furguson had seemed happy a few other times, those times were not so believable as this. If whatever you call beautiful makes you happy, then that's what beautiful things are for, I thought, especially if they belong to you. I wish, said Miss Furguson, that I could have given each of you a nice clean handkerchief to wipe your hands with before you entered this tearoom. If we were really in Japan, she said, that's what we'd do. I've invited Jolie Lotta to do the honors. We've rehearsed it together and we're pretty confident.

Then Jolie Lotta came forward and knelt down on a cushion, her bare knees touching the floor. She bowed her head to Miss Furguson, who knelt down, less easily, on the other cushion, and there they were, facing each other, their profiles to the class. I thought I might draw their picture together, later, as a way of being an important part of the ceremony, even almost necessary. To begin, said Miss Furguson, we must all admire the teapot and the bowls and even the bamboo whisk. They spent a long minute doing that, Miss Furguson making chirpy sounds of belief, of belief in the beauty of the objects set before them. With a small square of white silk, each one wiped the rim of her bowl so very much cleaner than any common cup was ever wiped. Then Jolie brought up from the floor a small iron kettle that had been waiting on a pad. Jolie, said Miss Furguson, is pouring the water slowly, very slowly, into the teapot which contains the green tea powder. Now, she said, Jolie is stirring it with the whisk. Too much stirring will make the tea foamy and too little will make the tea watery, so Jolie is stirring it just right, as you can see. Now the tea is steeping, said Miss Furguson. Then Jolie calmly, graciously, poured tea into Miss Furguson's bowl and into her own bowl, and wisps of steam rose up. How fragrant it is, said Miss Furguson, and they took their time inhaling. Then, at last, at last, they sipped their tea. Perfectly beautiful, said Miss Furguson. How perfect. And I knew that I would never draw them. My pen would make only false moves and the picture give away my lacking and my longing.

Nights at home, I thought about that tea ceremony. If Miss Furguson were ever to visit my family, something she'd never do but something I feared anyway, she'd know the worst if she came at suppertime. Her suspicions about us, and I knew she had some, would be confirmed before her eyes. Other families sat down together, while each member of my family ate apart. A family askew, a family alone in a rain-stained bungalow in the weeds, faded curtains from the last house that didn't fit the windows of this one, and my parents' bed a sagging fold-out davenport. My brother, who strode the streets all day or besieged our mother with dreams of fabulous wealth, ate by himself like a lone and hungry wolf, the first to be served by my sister. Over in Japan, he'd scare all those tea worshippers out of their wits. Teacups crashing to the floor, the teapot loudly cracking apart by itself. Our mother, who was served next, who ate more gracefully than anybody I'd ever seen but now sat with the dish in her lap and did not know exactly where in the dish to place her spoon, would never, of course, be invited. Next, my sweet sister and I sat down together, eating our supper just to get it over with, not talking, each knowing enough about what was in the other's unhappy heart. So afraid of making mistakes, my sister would not even be offered a chair where she could sit and watch the ceremony. My father came a long way on the clanking streetcar from the city, from his cluttered little office, and entered quietly, and did not sit down to eat until he had kissed our mother, gently, lovingly, on the top of her head. He placed only one thing at a time on his plate and ate slowly, and his shirt was white, washed and ironed by my sister, and our mother called him noble. My father, I thought, might possibly be acceptable at some celestial tea ceremony in some far distant time. One evening, coming in the door, he caught me doing something I had never done before, kneeling at my mother's slippered feet, begging her to tell me that someday I'd be a somebody. Tell me, tell me, I pleaded, and she waved her spoon over my head and said that I would. My father must have known, more than my mother did, what I meant by a somebody. A Somebody out in the world, who'd redeem us all.

One morning Miss Furguson stood up before us and told us something we already knew. We are at war, said Miss Furguson. The Japanese have bombed our territory, they have destroyed our ships, they have killed many of our sailors, and they have done this deceitfully.

The world went awry. It may always have been awry but I hadn't known, being so concentrated on my family awry. The world shattered itself, like that teapot my brother's presence would have caused to crack apart. Everywhere in the world millions of people were dying and great cities were blasted into rubble and dust and families huddled together in basements, hiding down there from inescapable night. Jolie Lotta disappeared from that class and her mother disappeared from the drugstore. I glanced in twice through the display window and could not find her.

Years into the war I began to look for something to call perfectly beautiful. Whatever it was, I couldn't find it again. I heard of a place in another city called a Museum of Art, and I wandered in. Carpets, like sanctification of my otherwise noisy shoes, and fragrance—sandalwood?—throughout the wide spaces, a fragrance I was to return for, again and again, as much as for the objects on their pedestals and in their frames. I stood before each one, or walked around it, at a loss. What I had to do, I saw, was imagine their beauty. What I had to do was dream it up, just what all those artists must have had to do. Wandering around in all that dreamed-up beauty, I thought about Jolie Lotta. How she presided at the tea ceremony, how she stirred the tea and poured it, and inhaled its fragrance, and drank it, and nodded in agreement with Miss Furguson that it was all perfectly beautiful, her own self, too, Jolie Lotta, amidst it all. If you could save yourself from a world awry by calling up something beautiful, I called up Jolie Lotta from my memory. Or I must have called her up from my wounded heart, since, even after so long, I wasn't spared the pain of my lacking and my longing.

# THE MISTRESS

It was not long after his arrival before he was introduced to her, but in that time she watched him from her vantage point that gave her a view of the long room filled with people, and, out the window, a view of the garden. She watched him because she knew at once, gazing down through the diamond panes, that he was the son of the man who had been her lover ten years ago, the son who had been six then. She knew, because the similarity was so striking she felt that she was gazing down upon the lover as he must have been at sixteen and at a moment when he had lifted his face to attempt an impassive scanning of the windows and found, in one, the face of a strange woman transfixed by him. She watched him enter the room, be kissed by the hostess, and thread his way between groups and couples, looking for no one in particular but only yearning, she suspected, to be halted, to be embraced, to be enclosed by some group and by the entire party. For several minutes he stood only a yard away from her, half-in and half-out of a group, holding his goblet of sherry and gazing down as if waiting for the wine to be joggled from his glass to the rug. He was tall, he was almost a man, he was on the verge of composure—she saw it alternate with discomfort, and his presence among adults, most of whom were strangers to him, reminded her of the legend of Theseus entering as a stranger the kingdom he was to rule someday.

She watched him because he was completely absorbing, combining as he did the familiar figure of the father with the enticing strangeness of the boy himself. She was thirty-six, the number of her husbands was three—the present one had been unable to attend the afternoon party—and the number of her lovers who had meant something to her was firmly fixed in her memory at one and that one was the father of the boy whom she was now spying on. The elderly man beside her on the bench was so enamored of her, his old black eyes glancing out untiringly from far inside the folds of eyelids at her crossed legs and bare, braceleted arms, that he was unaware of and therefore unhurt by her own glancing and gazing at someone else.

The boy was following the hostess as she went her rounds. Every joke, every anecdote being more amusing to her than to anybody else, she was constantly bending her knees to laugh, bending her body in the tight green dress, and for a time she used the boy as a partner in this dance of hers, grasping his arm and bending toward him until her forehead touched the pit of his stomach. But she was almost as small as an elf and whatever postures she adopted were not exaggerated, as they would be with a larger person, but simply made her presence known. Although he chatted eagerly enough with those she introduced him to, he always left them after a time to find the hostess again, as if nobody but she could give him a reason for being there, and when, at last, the hostess brought him over to her in her window, she knew as they approached that the hostess regarded her as perhaps the only person who could restrain the boy from his trailing.

So here was the boy, at last, the resemblance to his father defined less by closeness than by distance; now he was himself alto-gether, there was nothing that was a replica of his father, there were only sharp clues, a continual reminding. The elderly man to her right, rather than appear to be pushed off into oblivion by the two younger per-sons, rose with a sprightly tugging at tie and coat and offered to bring her another gin and tonic. She refused the offer charmingly, relieved and also reluctant to see him go, for any man's attentiveness was appreciated. She had always felt the need to thank the admirer for admiring.

"She's a good friend of my mother," he said, when they spoke of the hostess and her vivacity.

"Is your mother here?" she asked brightly, implying that if the son was so de-lightful a person to meet then the mother must also be met before the party was over.

He said that his mother was staying

with her sister in another city, and she wondered if the woman was being cared for by the sister, remembering that at one time during her affair with the boy's father, the wife had left, after a wild scene with him, and gone to her sister's, taking the child, and had been ill there for several weeks.

"Your father? Is he here?" she asked, knowing that he was in London and that he had transferred himself there four years ago, right after the divorce.

"He lives in London." The boy fumbled out a packet of matches from his coat pocket and lit her cigarette with a steady flame that compensated for his clumsiness. "I spent last summer over there."

"How is he?" she asked. "He was once a friend of mine." That innocuous information, when told to the son, was like a revelation of the truth. When recalled to the son, the memory of the father was as fresh and pervasive to her as if the affair had begun or ended only the day before.

"Great, great," the son said. "He's married again, and they've got a baby now, a little girl." She felt, listening, that the son and herself were both attached to him by love, by resentment, by all the responses of the ones left in the past of somebody of prominence and promise and with a life of his own, and who had no time or inclination for memories of past loves. "I wouldn't like living there all the time," he said. "London, that is," laughing in case she might think he meant living in his father's house.

"How does he look now?" she asked.

"Look?"

"Fatter, skinnier, gray or bald?"

"Oh, thinner, I'd say."

"Oh, yes, thinner," she cried, laughing. "He's the fibrous kind. They get tough like dried fruit." They let themselves go with laughing. Other guests glanced over at them, surprised by and disapproving of this sudden intrusion of laughter into the several conversations. "Gray yet?" she asked, arching her brows.

"No, no, not at all," he said. "Got fewer gray hairs than I do." A splash of sherry on her leg as he, clumsy with clowning, transferred the glass to riffle his hair with his right hand.

"Nothing," she assured him. "It's nothing." But the clumsiness reminded them of that insufficiency in the self, the manqué element that is felt by persons left in somebody else's past, persons who were not in step and who were dismayed by their falling behind. She saw that he was wondering about her—why she should laugh so eagerly over the present description of an old friend and why she could so easily compel him to join with her.

She rose, reaching down for his hand, all done in a moment as if he were doing the convincing and she was spontaneously amenable. "Come on, let's walk in the garden," she said over her shoulder as he followed her through the crowd, their hands linked. She turned her profile to him as they stood delayed by a congestion of guests near the door and spoke into his ear as he complyingly bent his head down. "When the air gets thick with smoke and gossip, I can't breathe," she whispered hoarsely, and, seeing him frown solicitously, baffled, as if she had named a rare disease, she patted his cheek to convey to him that her complaint wasn't serious. They each enjoyed the other's concern and, laughing about it, pushed out onto the wide arc of the brick steps.

She released his hand the moment they were in the open and took his elbow, instead, and swung along beside him with a movement in her hips more pronounced than she had tried for in a long time, yet wondering why her responses to the boy must be so extravagant. They crossed the bricks she had watched him cross and stepped out into the garden where other guests were walking the brick paths or sitting around the white, fancy ironwork tables. The flowers were so large and perfect that the garden seemed a greenhouse, and this illusion was intensified by the humid air.

"It reminds me of Mazatlán, this weather," she said. "The weeks before the rains came. Hot, hot, everybody out along the beaches, the esplanade, till way past midnight, children and everybody. I remember the night the storm came, the first storm. The little trees by the window were

bent over horizontal and the lightning con-
tinuous, sheets of lightning, and the rain
and the wind, and the coolness coming
into the windows, but the air still warm. I
remember I went out into it, wrapped my
raincoat over me and went out, but someone looking out a window told me to get
back in, it was dangerous—the lightning,
and the rain all over the ground in a flood."
She glanced away. "The sand there is pink
and gold, and weird birds—I guess they're
vultures of some sort—hover over the
beach. At night you can see the lights of La
Paz across the water, or think you can. Your
father was there at the time. He was there,
too. In Mazatlán."

"Did you meet him there?" he asked.

"We knew each other before," she said,
and was impatient to reveal to him a woman
from out of his father's life, a woman he had
not known existed, impatient to compel him

to see her as he would imagine his father had seen her and to experience for a time, for the rest of the day, what she had meant to his father. Impatient to re-create the father and herself, the lovers. With her head bowed over a yellow leaf she had picked up, she strolled down the path a step ahead of him to contend with her urge to reveal to him that which ought to be left in the father's past and in her own.

"I remember he went to Mexico when I was six," he said. "He wrote me a letter. I was just learning to write and I answered him. He kept my letter. My mother has it. God, the spelling!"

"He went there with me," she said. "Or I went with him. We were lovers."

She had told him in order to experience again, as she was doing now as he followed her, the delight of being both desired and desirous as she had known it then. She had told him in order to experience again that greater awareness of herself, of the shifting and floating of the weightless silk around her thighs, of the threads of her hair that, glimpsed from the corner of her eye, were like flying spider silk in the sun, seen and not seen. She had told him in order to experience again that woman she had been years ago, followed by the man, the father. When he came alongside her she glanced at him to see her effect upon him, and saw the face of a sick child.

They stood in the shade of trees; and all things, the fragrance of the flowers, the tang of the limes from the drinks on a table close by, the voices in conversation among the trees and flowers, the heat of the day, some dust in the air from somewhere on the other side of the high, wrought-iron fence, everything served to make his face that of a boy taken sick at a picnic. "I remember you," he said, pressing at the leaves on the path with his heel. "I don't mean that I met you. I just mean that I remember you."

"How?" she asked.

"The time, I mean," he said. "I remember the time."

"The time?" She felt the loss of herself, as if she no longer existed even in anyone's memory, her features, her voice, all forgotten. Only the time remained as a frame empty of its picture of a woman.

"My mother used to cry," he explained. "She seemed to be crying all the time. And they would quarrel when he came home. The mascara would run down her cheeks and make black tears."

"But they weren't getting along even before he met me."

"Yes, I suppose," he said. "But she cried anyway about you."

He lifted his eyes in the silence he had

enforced, and they were a child's accus-
ing eyes, the eyes of a boy troubled by his
mother's troubles, seeing his mother's face
streaked by the mascara, hearing the quar-
reling through a wall, through a door left
open.

"You shouldn't have told me," he said.

"Or committed the crime ten years
ago?"

"No, no, I know more about people
now," he said, defending his store of wisdom. "I just said you shouldn't have said
it," trying to tell her that he was ashamed
for reacting as a child, thrusting his mother
between them, and that she should not have
forced him back into the past, into the child
loyal to the mother, when he was enjoying
her company, the company of a strange
woman who was giving him her time and
gracefulness and wit, gifts that implied his
maturity.

The shame he felt for reacting as a child and the love aroused for his mother struggled together, denying him any further ease with her. They walked side by side past guests who fell silent as they went silently by, much like lovers who have had their concluding quarrel. They made a circle of the garden, and at the table nearest the porch she stopped to chat with a friend. The boy went on before she could introduce him, and, glancing after him, she saw him striding down the driveway and out the wide-open gate.

The woman she was chatting with drew out from behind her a round, yellow cushion and tossed it into the empty chair. She sat down and continued the chatting, smoking and smiling, and seeing the face of his mother weeping black, bitter tears. She sat with her bare arms on the table, observing how the circle of trees and the soft, pointillistic light through the leaves all gave the group around the table the intimacy of a group in a painting, but seeing, all the time, the face of the weeping woman. There was unhappiness and tears for that woman long before she, the mistress, appeared in their lives, there was nothing that could have been done even if this feeling for the other woman had been experienced at that time, but her indifference, then, struck her now as a failing. She felt that she was a hundred years old, at last discovering that the person in her memory who affected her the most was not the one she had loved the most but the one she had understood the least.

She turned partly away and, reaching over the back of her chair, picked a leaf from a small tree blossoming with purple flowers, and with this activity concealed her face from the woman with whom she'd been talking.

# THE OVERCOAT

The overcoat was black and hung down to his ankles, the sleeves came down to his fingertips, and the weight of it was as much as two overcoats. It was given him by an old girlfriend who wasn't his lover anymore but stayed around just to be his friend. She had chosen it out of a line of Goodwill coats because, since it had already lasted almost a century, it was the most durable and so the right one for his trip to Seattle, a city she imagined as always flooded by cataclysmic rains and cold as an execution dawn. His watch cap came down to his eyebrows.

On the Trailways bus the coat overlapped onto the next seat, and only when all other seats were occupied did a passenger dare to lift it and sit down, women apologetically, men bristling at the coat's invasion of their territory. The coat was formidable. Inside it he was frail. His friend had filled a paper bag with delicatessen items, hoping to spare him the spectacle of himself at depot counters, hands shaking, coffee spilling, a sight for passengers hungrier for objects of ridicule than for their hamburgers and French fries. So he sat alone in the bus while it cooled under the low ceilings of concrete depots and out in lots under the winter sky, around it piles of wet lumber, cars without tires, shacks, a chained dog, and the café's neon sign trembling in the mist.

On the last night, the bus plowed through roaring rain. Eli sat behind the driver. Panic might take hold of him any moment and he had to be near a door, even the door of this bus crawling along the ocean floor. No one sat beside him, and the voices of the passengers in the dark bus were like the faint chirps of birds about to be swept from their nest. In the glittering tumult of water beyond the swift arc of the windshield wiper, he was on his way to see his mother and his father, and panic over his sight of them and over their sight of him might wrench him out of his seat and lay him down in the aisle. He pressed his head against the cold glass and imagined escaping from the bus and from his parents, revived or destroyed out there in the icy deluge.

For three days he lay in a hotel room, unable to face the two he had come so far to see and whom he hadn't seen in sixteen years, the age he'd been when he'd seen them last. They were already old when he was a kid, at least in his eyes, and now they seemed beyond age. The room was cold and clammy, but he could have sworn a steam radiator was on, hissing and sputtering. Then he figured an old man was sitting in a corner, watching over him, sniffling and sadly whistling. Until he took the noise by surprise and caught it coming from his own mouth, an attempt from sleep to give an account of himself.

Lying under the hotel's army blanket and his overcoat, he wished he had waited until summer. But all waiting time was dangerous. The worst you could imagine always happened to you while you were waiting for better times. Winter was the best time for him, anyway. The overcoat was an impenetrable cover for his wasted body, for his arms lacerated by needles, scar on scar, like worms coming out, with the tattoos like road maps to show them the way. Even if it were summer he'd wear the overcoat. The sun would have to get even fiercer than in that story he'd read when he was a kid, about the sun and the wind betting each other which of them could take off the man's coat, and the sun won. Then he'd take off his coat, he'd even take off his shirt, and his parents would see who'd been inside. They'd see Eli under the sun.

With his face bundled up in a yellow plaid muffler he'd found on the floor of the bus, he went by ferry and by more buses way out to the edge of this watery state, avoiding his mother by first visiting his father. Clumping in his navy surplus shoes down to the fishing boats riding the glacial gray sea, he was thrown off course by panic, by the presence of his father in one of those boats, and he zigzagged around the little town like an immense black beetle, blown across the ocean from its own region.

On the deck of his father's boat he was instantly dizzied by the lift and fall and the jolting against the wharf, and he held to the rail of the steep steps down to the cabin, afraid he was going to be thrown onto his father, entangling them in another awful mishap.

"Eli. Eli here," he said.

"Eli?"

"That's me," he said.

Granite, his father had turned to granite. The man sitting on the bunk was gray, face gray, skimpy hair gray, the red net of broken capillaries become black flecks, and he didn't move. The years had chiseled him down to nowhere near the size he'd been.

"Got arthritis," his father said. The throat, could it catch arthritis, too? His voice was the high-pitched whisper of a woman struggling with a man, it was Eli's mother's voice, changed places. "Got it from the damn wet, took too many falls. Got it since you been gone."

The Indian woman beside him shook tobacco from a pouch, rolled the cigarette, licked it closed, and never looked up. "You got it before he went," she said, and to Eli, "How long you been gone? A couple weeks?"

"Sixteen years, more or less."

"Eli's my son," his father said.

The Indian woman laughed. "I thought you were Louie. Got a boat next to ours. We been expecting him. Got to tell him his shortwave radio was stolen. Storm did some damage, too. You Harry's son? He never told me. You a fisherman like your dad?"

"Nope."

"He's smart," his father said.

"Never got a kick out of seeing all those fishes flopping around in the net, fighting for their lives."

"Eli always saw stuff that wasn't going on," his father said. "That kid never saw what was real. Did you?"

"Never did," said Eli.

"You want to sit?" his father asked.

Eli sat on the bunk opposite them.

"That's a big overcoat you got there," his father said. "You prosperous?"

"I'm so prosperous I got a lot of parasites living off me."

"They relatives of yours?" she asked.

"Anything living off you is a relative," he said.

"I'm never going to live off you and you're never going to live off me," his father said.

"Right," said Eli.

"You visit your mom?" the woman asked.

"Not yet. I don't know where she is."

"Nobody," said his father, "could ever

figure that out. A rest home for the time being. She lived too fast and hard, got to rest for a while. What a woman. A redhead. They burn up themselves."

"What color's *your* hair?" the woman asked.

Eli took off his watch cap.

"What happened to your hair? You're kind of bald for a guy young as you."

"Fell out."

"That's the way them punks wear their hair," his father said.

"I've been sick, that's why," he said.

"Are you hungry?" she asked.

"Can't say."

"I got some beans left in the pan, would you like that?"

"Thanks. Can't say," he said.

The woman pushed herself up in stages, her weight giving her a hard time, like a penalty. She wore a mackinaw and men's trousers and two pairs of thick socks, the holes in the top pair showing the socks underneath. Her breasts hung to her waist though she had no waist, but when she lifted her arms to light a hanging kerosene lamp he saw how gracefully she did it, her hands acting like a pretty girl's. He could have fallen for her himself when he was sixteen.

On the narrow table between the bunks she set down a battered pan and a large spoon. He scooped up a few beans, found them too much to deal with, and put the spoon back in the pan.

"Guess I'm not hungry, thanks," he said. "What I need is a place to sleep. Just for tonight. I used to sleep on this bunk when I was a kid."

"It's nice you remember," she said.

"Go ahead and lie down. See if you still fit," his father said.

"I'll wait 'til everybody's in bed."

"The army ever get you?" his father asked.

"Never got me, didn't want me."

"That's good they didn't want you," she said.

"What's wrong with the army?" his father said. "What the hell else did you do with your life?"

"You talk like his life is over," the woman said. "He's young. He's just a little older than my boy Nate."

"I wrecked it," Eli said. "You detected the secret of my life."

"Well now you see you got sick," his father said. "Could be you're being punished for wrecking your life."

"Could be," Eli said.

"Go ahead and lie down," his father said. "You look like you're about to drop dead. What do the doctors say?"

"Just what you said."

Eli lay down, wrapping his overcoat more closely around himself.

"You want me to take your shoes off?" she asked. "I got some extra socks, they'll keep your feet warm."

"No thanks, I'll be fine," he said, pulling his watch cap down over his ears and his eyes.

"We sleep aft," she said. "If you need anything, just call. My name's Myrna."

Outside his cap things went dark. She must have snuffed out the lamp. He lay in his overcoat, drawing his legs up close against his hollow stomach. Then he imagined he was a boy again, home again in the house in Seattle, under covers in his own bed while his parents drank the night away, unprotected from them but protected by them from the dreadful world they said was out there. Then he thought about the strangers he'd met, out in that world. The ones who said *Tell me about your parents, Eli*, the ones who said they were there to help him. Smirky parole officers and smug-faced boy psychologists in leather jackets, jiving with him like a cellmate, and that female social worker in her short skirt, whose thighs he'd hope to open with the shining need for love in his eyes. *In the morning of your life*. That was the way she'd put it. It made him go weak in the head, he'd say anything she wanted him to say, and he'd blamed this old man on this rotting boat and he'd blamed his mother, wherever she was, for what had become of Eli. They had pried out his heart, those prying strangers, and the empty place left behind was where death got in. He knew this for a fact.

At dawn he was wakened by his shivering body. Out on the pier, the cold salt wind stiffened him, almost blinding him, so that he wound up a few times at the pier's edges.

When you look back, he'd heard, you're turned into salt, and that's what was happening to him. If he fell into the sea he'd disappear faster than he was bound to already.

For two days he wandered Seattle. Now that he was near to his mother he wanted to go on by. He had betrayed her, he had blamed her for Eli. Somebody was to blame and he didn't know who. If his father was right, then Eli was to blame for what he'd done to himself, and proof was in the punishment. Once and for all, Eli was to blame.

They told him at the desk that his mother was ambulatory and could be anywhere. The old women in the rows of narrow beds, and the women in their chairs between the beds, hadn't much left of womanness in them, but their power over him was intact. He went along before their pale faces staring out at the last puzzling details of the world, himself a detail, a cowering man in a long black overcoat, who might be their long-lost father, come to visit.

There she was, far down a corridor and out, and he followed her into a paved yard, walled in by brick and concrete. She put her hand to the wall to aid herself in open space, reached the bench and sat down, and her profile assured him he wasn't mistaken.

"Mother, it's Eli," he said, taking off his watch cap.

She raised her eyes, and one eye was shrewdly narrowed and the other as purely open as a child's, the blue almost as blue as ever.

"Eli," he said. "Can I sit down?"

"Room enough for everybody."

He sat, and she paid him no attention.

The day was cold, but she had come out wearing only a sagging sweater, a skirt, pink socks, and sluffy shoes. From a pocket of her sweater she took a scrap of comb and began to comb her hair. The comb went cautiously through the tangle of flame-red and gray curls.

"Mother, I'm Eli," he said. "Eli, your only child."

"You're right about that," she said. "Had one and that was it. Well, no. Had another but lost it in the womb. Fell down or was pushed. Things come and go. I figure they go more often than they come. Not much came my way but I lost more than I had. If you see what I mean."

"Mother, I wish I'd stayed around," he said. "I wouldn't let him hurt you anymore."

"Who hurt me?"

"Dad did."

"Oh, him? Once in a blue moon I get a postcard. One time he visited but I was ashamed of him. He walks like an old dog with something wrong in his hind end."

"Mother, don't be afraid to look at me."

"I don't see as good as I used to," she explained. "In the past I used to read the teeniest print. When I was a girl, believe me, I was the smartest in my class. The best looking, too. It wasn't just my red hair, it was more. I was wild to begin. That and my hair drove everybody wild. It's contagious."

"Look at me," he begged. "Come across."

She drew the sweater over her breasts and kept her arms crossed there. "We had ourselves an earthquake today. Did you feel it? Bricks fell down. We thought the whole damn place was coming down."

"I wasn't here."

"Were you scared?"

"I wasn't here."

"Go on. I bet you were scared."

"I died in it," he said. If she wanted his company in her earthquake it was no trouble to oblige. It made no difference, afterwards, when or where you died, and it was easier to tell her he was already dead than tell her he was going to be soon, maybe even before he could get up from this bench.

Slowly she turned her head to take a close look at him, this man who had sat down beside her to belittle her with his lie. "You never died," she said. "You're alive as me. I saw to it. Nothing got by me. Awful things happen to boys out there. I'd wake up in the middle of the night, sure somebody was out to harm you that exact second. I'd yell, 'Run, Eli, run! I'll take care of this fiend!' And that's how I rescued you, every time."

"You did. Every time," he said.

Off in a corner, facing the wall, he covered his head with the overcoat and in that dark tent wept, baffled by them, by the woman over there on the bench, combing her hair again, and by the old man on the rocking boat. They were baffled by what had gone on in their lives and by what was going on now and by whatever was to go on, and this was all they had to offer him, Eli, come back to them, baffled enough by his own life.

# STOLEN PLEASURES

Every house had a palm tree and a lawn, and some had a piano inside, a dark, sternly upright object in its own realm called the living room. Delia and her family had no piano and therefore no living room. Living, their kind, went on everywhere in their house, smaller than the other houses and closer to the alley. It was the piano that made a room into a living room, because the piano, she figured, promised the children of the family happy lives to come if only they'd learn to play it.

The piano, a huge, flat, forbidding face,

until her best friend, Ellsworth, across the alley, sat down before it, lifted the long upper lip, baring the long rows of black and yellow teeth clamped together in an unsightly grin, and with nervous fingers picked out cajoling sounds that meant *Please, piano, piano, open up a happy future for me, for me, piano, please, for me, for me.*

Inside, where you couldn't see what was going on, a lot of little hammers were beating on strings. A hidden cruelty in there, it seemed to Delia, slumped down on the floor in a corner, chewing on the untied strings at the neck of her soiled dress. Without a piano, were her parents doubtful of her and her sister's future? Would they die while children? That very year, while Delia was seven, she was struck by a car, and her hair had to be cut short and away from the wound that became a scar the size of a silver dollar behind her ear, and that very year, her sister, Fleur, fourteen, came down with scarlet fever, and Delia spent gentle hours in bed with her, peeling away the shedding skin. Could they both have died that very year because they had no piano? While Ellsworth's small fingers begged the piano for a future happier than hers, she picked grass off her bare, dirty feet and tauntingly wished for his mother to come home and find her there, his undesirable best friend.

When she grew up, Delia still saw herself as outside the realm of music. And if you were a man interested enough to take her out on a date and talk to her about a famous pianist or sax player or a concert you'd been to, you'd wonder why she couldn't look you in the eyes at that point and why she got clumsy, knocking a fork to the floor or tipping over her wineglass.

For a time there was a violin in the house that had no piano. Fleur never really asked for the violin, she never asked for anything, and so the granting of the violin seemed only to comply with the high school principal's decree that every student learn a musical instrument. The only thing Fleur ever asked for was a pair of glasses so she could read the blackboard at school. She was lagging far behind the other students and ridiculed by them and even by the teachers. She asked their father each semester, and he said neither yes nor no, and when she was already fifteen she told him she'd drown herself in the ocean, it was only a mile away, and then she was granted glasses. Delia, too small then to know the depths of frustration in her sister's breast and in her father's head, learned only later from Fleur when she was old enough to know. But the night their father brought the violin home and Fleur opened the case and lifted it from the green velvet lining, for that moment Fleur, too, was assured a happy future.

Virginia, Ellsworth's sister and Fleur's best friend, came across the alley to take a look at the violin. Since her father, she said, played the organ in church and her mother sang in the choir, and she herself played the violin and the piano both, Fleur could never hope to catch up, though there was no harm in trying. Was it winter and early dark, that evening?

Once Delia followed Fleur to her violin lesson down the street and stood outside to see how Mrs. Chase opened the door and let her sister in. Without a smile, Mrs. Chase stepped back and in went Fleur, head bowed, careful not to bang the violin case against anything, especially not against a woman so plumply elegant, her dress of large flowers and gathers, her blond hair drawn smoothly back to reveal her whole pale, prettified face.

Fleur practiced at night after she'd done her homework, though their father turned the lights out at half past nine. Not just a time called a Depression, called Dark Times, not just the War and the blackouts (if a light showed through a tear in your window shade you'd be guilty of the deaths of thousands), not just a father denies you the light to learn something by. Fleur began to deny it to herself.

Fleur carried notes from their mother to Mrs. Chase, promising to pay, notes she had to write herself because their mother couldn't write as well as Fleur, whose handwriting was perfect penmanship, slanting always in the right direction like a constant catching up. Fleur didn't cry when the lessons came to an end. Delia saw Fleur cry only once and that one time was in the years to come. That one time was when Delia was fourteen and in high school and Fleur was already twenty-one, and they were living in an even barer house somewhere else, and their father was dead. Fleur's wish to go to the School for Nurses, far from home, where she was accepted and where she could live and where Virginia already was, that wish was drowned that day in the flood of tears and Fleur was carried away with it. She was to spend all the years of her young life tending their mother and doing the tasks a mother does. Fleur sat in a room by herself, crying for hours, and nobody went in to her though the door was open. Delia didn't go in, she was afraid to go in.

When Delia was very little, three, four years old, and Fleur went off to school on a day of high winds, then Delia would stand by the window and pray that her sister not be swept away. Even then, Delia sensed a waiting emptiness in Fleur that might never be filled with experiences other girls were to have. It set her apart from the girls she walked to school with. She'd be the one the winds would carry off.

When Delia was seven, with a voice of her own, she became her sister's protector, chastising grocery clerks and strange men, whoever happened to notice how one of Fleur's eyes slid upward whenever it felt like it. "Do you know your eye's crooked?" they said, and "Can't you look straight at me?" and the shock of their demands did bring it down. Holding Fleur's hand, she shouted, "You don't ask that question!" She told them to leave her sister alone, she told them to mind their own business.

When their mother went for strolls in the evening, Delia went with her, and, passing Ellsworth's house, they heard the piano and the violin at the same time, and even Mrs. Walshman singing. Fleur always stayed home, figuring out her homework and cutting pictures out of magazines and pasting them in a scrapbook, and when the stroll was over and they came into their little house, there was Fleur at their only table, pasting things without ripples, writing under the picture what it was: A Castle in Spain, A Movie Star, A Bouquet. Under the lamplight she was beautiful in Delia's eyes, a girl with auburn curls and large brown eyes, a girl who'd come quietly there when they were away.

Delia was afraid to wonder if Fleur was not loved by their parents as much as she was. That imbalance was like a burden on Delia. It wasn't enough that their parents had named Fleur after a heroine in a romantic novel that their father read to their mother, evenings, while she was carrying Fleur inside her. Something more was needed. She asked Fleur if she loved their parents, afraid that if she did not she'd be punished by God. Fleur, whose faint frowns always seemed over something else, said that she did.

Once Delia took the violin from the closet and carefully looked it over to see why it had failed to bring to Fleur the same kind of future as Virginia's. The very shape of it, and the glossy wood, and the curlicues, and the tiny wooden bridge that held up the strings—how untouchably perfect it must seem to Fleur who was so cast down by her shortcomings and mistakes. That night at the table cleared of supper things, Delia sat across from Fleur and drew the violin on a piece of her sister's lined tablet paper, and drew her sister playing it, bow in hand.

"Is that me?" said Fleur. "It looks like a little ant I saw playing Mrs. Chase's violin. She said it had no future and crushed it dead."

Fleur's hesitant jokes surprised people,

but they never took Delia by surprise because Delia knew what Fleur had inside herself to say when the chance came.

A hint of a bountiful future touched Fleur once more as the violin had seemed to do. When Fleur took Delia to a movie matinee, Fleur's ticket won a complete set of sherbet goblets. Delia would hold one up to the light and imagine that someday they'd live in a very nice house where the amber goblets would really belong. Only tapioca pudding was eaten from them. Years later, when their mother died and Fleur came to live with Delia in her apartment in San Francisco, she brought along the three that were left of the goblets, and for the very first time in their lives they ate sherbet.

"Sherbet is what the very rich eat between courses," Delia said. "It cools their mouths, it sort of cleanses their taste for the next thing. I read that somewhere." It wasn't something she'd read, it was told her by a lover who knew a lot about what the rich did, but there was no point in telling her sister that small truth. Fleur was like truth itself and other truths were negligible.

A Black Sheep. Their mother said their father was a Black Sheep, and so did his two brothers, who came once to visit. They wore suits that had no wrinkles, and Delia guessed that their shirts were not washed and ironed by a wife or a daughter, as her father's shirts were, but by someone not part of the family. They must have grown older faster than her father. Their faces were creased, their hair already gray, while her father's hair was dark and curly all around his bald spot. One brother was a furrier, the other a jeweler, but they brought neither furs nor jewels. They brought only their Black Sheep tag for this youngest brother, who put his head to the side and smiled, too, over what they called him. So a Black Sheep was not so bad a thing to be, if he could smile over it.

The brothers looked around in a way that seemed not looking, not interested, that saw emptiness where there was no overstuffed couch and no rugs and no piano and no real living room. They did not look at Delia, but they looked at Fleur, who did not look even once at them, and they saw more than Delia had seen before and opened to her eyes her sister's long shapely legs and high breasts and what appeared to be Fleur's desire to conceal herself. A desire that was modesty, her father explained to his brothers, which made them smile once more.

Silent critics of their brother, they diminished everything down to what they'd expected of a Black Sheep. If Delia's father had wanted something from them, it wasn't given. The brothers had come from Denver, where their old mother, who was in her nineties, and their father, who was even older and who went to a synagogue every day to praise God, lived in a large house of three stories. Once in a while Delia heard her parents mention her father's sister, Sophie, but she seemed to be dead.

Their father said he was born "at the turn of the century," and his family in Denver, he said, didn't know that when one century comes to an end, another century begins, and times change, and people's thinking changes. His family, he said, was stuck in the Past. His brothers were married to very rich and homely women, sisters, who didn't invite him into their homes when he was visiting his family.

Delia's mother was always charmingly lively around people, even those she didn't know. She was born in a very small

country over in Europe, whose name neither Fleur nor Delia could remember when
teachers asked where their parents were
born. When Delia did remember, she was
ashamed to say it because nobody had ever
heard of it. Aunt Goldie, their mother's sister, and her daughter, Cousin Jean, came
once in a while when their father wasn't
home. They drove up in a big Packard,
bringing chocolates and cookies, Jean in
furs and diamonds given to her by a gen-
erous man who was in the movies, in ex-
change, their mother said, for Jean's own
kind of generosity, her plumpness and her
kisses and high spirits. Jean tried to teach
Fleur the fox-trot, but Fleur kept looking down at her feet to make them mind,
and they wouldn't, and Delia, trying, too,
wasn't much better at it because she was
watching Fleur to help her out. Delia tried
to listen to the song Jean was humming,

but it was a song just for people who knew how to dance to it.

Their father told their mother about intelligent men he had interesting talks with, and so Delia hoped he had friends away from home, probably at the company where he was a printer, friends who simply never had time to come to visit. Together with their mother he had one friend at home, but since Mr. Bonner was their mother's friend, too, and called her Eva, and came by to see her when their father was away, he could not be confirmed as more their father's than their mother's friend. He and their father talked together in the yard and shook hands whenever they met, and he called their father by his first name, Maurice, though their father called him only Mr. Bonner.

Mr. Bonner honored them by coming to their house, while other bankers were to be seen only at their desks. He always wore a suit the color of cream, a Stetson hat the same color, and his shoes were always polished, and not, Delia was sure, by his wife, as her father's were, every night. Taller than her father, who was stocky and whose chest was broad and who had a bushy mustache and wore a cap and a wrinkled brown suit from a department store basement, Mr. Bonner stood stolidly high, his face smooth as a woman's, his eyes so palely blue Delia wondered if her father's brown eyes could see more.

Mr. Bonner sang whispery songs just for himself to hear. Sometimes, when Mr. Bonner came to see their mother, she would leave what she was doing and go off with him, telling Fleur she was coming back very soon. She wore just her housedress and her legs were bare, a tall slender woman with dark, bobbed hair. One dress that Delia was to remember had little orange flowers in the print of it.

On one of those afternoons when their mother was gone, Delia persuaded Fleur to come with her into the front house where the oil workers lived and who were away at work on Signal Hill. They always left their back door open, the screen door banging away in a warm wind all day. Delia's mother, who was their landlady, called the oil workers by their first names and cleaned their house and made their beds for them. On Sunday afternoons when their girlfriends were visiting, Delia went in and accepted oranges and Oreo cookies and pretended she wasn't watching the way their girlfriends smoked, how they held their cigarettes and how they crossed their legs.

Fleur came reluctantly, that day, to the oil workers' house. Like her housekeeping

mother, Delia picked up coins from the bedroom rug and set them in an honest row on
the dresser top. That seemed a good deed to
Fleur, who picked up a round, golden com-
pact and set it alongside the coins.

Delia said, "Open it up," and Fleur
would not, so Delia did. The cake of rouge
was a rose petal larger than any real one.

Delia swept the kitchen floor. Then she
went on into the living room, directly to the
phonograph, and lifted the lid.

"You shouldn't do that," said Fleur.

Wanting to hear for herself the music
the pretty women danced to, Delia set the
needle down at the edge of the record. The
music blared out without a beginning and
didn't go back to start over. It came faster
than other music and was made by many
people who all seemed to know that what
they wanted from life was just what they'd
get, and much more, and soon, even right

that instant. Her mother had said it was Jazz. The music invited her in and pushed her out. The music was the property of the pretty women who kicked off their high heels and swished their skirts around their hips and threw themselves down on the oil workers' laps. She lifted the arm to make the music stop, but the arm got away from her small sneaky hand and cut a long willful scratch across the record.

Years later, when she came to live with Delia, Fleur, bothered by memories imposed on her just as their life back then had been imposed on her, asked Delia, out of the blue, "Do you remember Mr. Bonner?"

Delia said that she did. She remembered that Mr. Bonner had visited one time after they'd moved, when their mother was already blind, and that a few years later a letter had come from his son, telling them that his father had died.

"Do you remember that quarrel Mama and Papa had?"

Fleur, asking that question, opened up for Delia the realization that the quarrel between their mother and father, their only quarrel she'd ever heard, was not really about politics, as she'd always thought. Their father had just come home, he was sitting in a chair, taking off his shoes, and he was saying that Mr. Bonner called union organizers wild-eyed Reds, that Mr. Bonner was a leech, that it wasn't the meek who were going to inherit the earth. Fleur and Delia, trembling on the other side of the half-open door, were told to go away.

"What makes you remember that quarrel now?" Delia asked.

"I don't know," said Fleur.

But Delia knew. By bringing up that scene, Fleur was divulging at last her long-ago wondering about their mother's stolen pleasures. Within a year or so after that quarrel, they lost their little house and the house where the oil workers lived, and moved to a lying-low kind of house that wasn't theirs, that was next door to a squab farm, from where the feathers off the poor caged birds drifted over and down onto their beds and bare floors. That's where they were when their father died, and that's where they were when darkness closed in around their mother, and she sat before her little radio, listening to the serial romances and waving her hand before her eyes, hoping to see it take shape again out of the dark, and when she couldn't bear the dark anymore she tore at her face, and they struggled with her to hold down her arms, Fleur on one side, Delia on the other. That's where they were, still, when their mother's hands began to twist up, her hair turn stiff and gray, her body become hard peaks and hollows under the blankets, and that's where they were when Fleur must have given up wondering, almost forever but not forever, what stolen pleasures were all about.

One night when they were undressing in Delia's apartment, by their two single beds, Fleur, her back turned, modest even in the presence of her own sister, said, "I want to tell you something," and waited until they were both under their covers and Delia had switched off the lamp between them.

"When you began to stay out all night, do you remember?"

"I remember," said Delia.

"Do you remember how Mama used to say you were like Sophie?"

Their mother had said it from her bed, aware in her darkness that Delia was slipping on her coat. Who knew when Delia would come back and who knew what she did when she was away? *Sophie had terrible moods, like you. Sophie made trouble for everybody, like you. You just came home this morning, why can't you stay and rest?* And what had Delia answered, shocking herself with that answer? "I'll rest in my grave," she had said, and saw how it shocked their mother, too, this gripping sense of mortality in a girl so young.

"You never thought how hard it was on me," said Fleur.

Delia had lost touch with Fleur in those years of her desire for the love of men, those years of humiliating herself for men in the hope of proving unforgettably precious to them.

"When you stayed out all night, Mama said terrible things were going to happen to you. She never slept. Nights were like nightmares for me. I told you but you didn't care. Then you left me alone with her forever when you came here."

Then Fleur turned away. She had so much to say it could be said only a little at a time.

At certain times in the night, Fleur's breathing took on the sound of sorrow kept down in her breast. Of sorrow that her young life had been taken from her while she'd hoped it was yet to come. And Delia said to her sleeping sister: I had to leave, I had to find my own life, but it was never and may not ever be the life you thought I was enjoying. Mean things happened to me I never told you about. Not terrible things like Mama said were going to happen, just mean things that make life itself seem mean and you wonder why you're living it. I took a job where I did the dishes and polished the silver, and for that I got a room near the kitchen, and so I didn't have to pay rent any- where and I could send money to you to add a little to what Papa's relatives sent. I'd come home there from my other jobs, and one night when I was drying the dishes, the family kids, a boy and a girl, twelve, thirteen, kids with cold hearts, used the dish towels like whips and slapped me in the face with them. I put my hands over my face, that's all. I used to be your defender when I was a kid, I used to fight back for you, but I couldn't do it for myself.

Delia took Fleur to the museums. Culture meant that you could fill the emptiness of your life with marvelous things that were out there for everyone to share in. They wandered over the marble floors, attempting interest in the paintings and the sculpture and the rooms of historical furniture, Fleur soon wearied by her incomprehension of so many objects of value. There was always one woman in the museum throngs, or a child, who kept glancing at Fleur to figure her out: her refugee look, her sacrificial look, her look of displacement. No one could ever even hope to know where Fleur came from.

She took Fleur to a bookstore a friend had told her about, where you could look at handmade books that were works of art, the words of famous writers exquisitely printed on the finest papers you would ever see. Collectors paid a lot for them, her friend said. Distant, delicate guitar music seemed to be inviting into the store even those not about to buy anything. A woman came out of her office, suspicious of these two who must look abashed by their own selves, like thieves who had just stolen something from somewhere else. Delia sensed Fleur moving back in fear from Mrs. Chase, who had never been paid for those last violin lessons.

Taking Fleur's hand, such a small hand for an older sister, Delia urged her on to the array of open books along the shelves.

Fleur took her glasses from her purse and put them on, using them as an invitation to touch a page.

"It's a poem," said Fleur.

"There are gloves for that," said the watching woman, and so there were. A basketful of white cotton gloves. "If you don't put them on you'll have to leave. I'd rather you leave."

Shakily, Fleur put her glasses away.

"My sister's hands are clean," said Delia. "You're the one who shouldn't touch."

They left, Fleur's head bent, Delia's high.

"People always looked down on us," Fleur said that night.

"Not everybody," said Delia.

"Everybody."

"That's an awful way to think."

"Papa's family did," said Fleur. "They looked down on us. Papa said they were so strict, how they had separate plates for milk things and separate plates for meat. I used to think they looked down on us because we didn't have separate plates."

Delia waited.

"That wasn't why," said Fleur.

"It was because he was a Black Sheep, that's why," said Delia.

"You remember the night they took Papa away to that charity hospital?" said Fleur. "I went with him because Mama couldn't and I was the oldest and you stayed with her, and in the ambulance they said he'd better sit up, that was best if you had a heart attack. I held his hand. He was cold but he was sweating, and I thought he was sweating because he was afraid he was going to die. When we got there they wouldn't take him up to the ward until he answered questions. I wished the nurse would stop asking so they could take him up and take care of him. He was sitting up like they told him to and his chest was bare, it was glistening. The nurse was asking him what his mother's maiden name was, and he said it was Taubes, and she said No, that's your name, that's not your mother's maiden name, and he said it again, and finally she took down that name. I thought he gave her his own name because he was so afraid he was going to die he couldn't think of the name she wanted."

Delia tried to recall how old Fleur was, that night their father died. Eighteen? That night, years ago, Fleur had found her way home from that distant hospital, showing up at dawn. Delia, afraid that Fleur was lost, was gone forever along with their father, stood away from her when she appeared at last. Stood away in grief for Fleur and for their father, both. Pale Fleur, saddened by life and by death.

"I went up to where he was," said Fleur. "He told me he wanted a drink of water, and I told the nurse but she said he wasn't allowed any water, and she told me to go home. I didn't go. I stayed out in the hall and I looked at him from far and he could see me. I think I saw when he died."

Fleur turned to face the wall.

They did not go to concerts, not even to the free concerts in the public groves. Nor did they go into the churches where you could sit in a pew and watch the choirs sing or listen to the organ. Music in churches was for those who saw God differently than the way Delia saw Him. They had a radio but seldom turned it on. Once, in a store, Delia caught sight of an entire orchestra on a large television screen, and she paused to watch. The pianist, under the grand piano's slanting wing, was grimacing as if in pain, and so were some of the other musicians, as if they were striving to keep up, as if the performance was an ordeal. She did not hear the music, she was put off by the faces. Some musicians Delia passed on the street, carrying their black instrument cases, seemed troubled by a problem she'd never know anything about, unless it was about making a living, and that one she knew very well.

A friend, a man who had been her lover, gave Delia two tickets to a concert at the Opera House, tickets that had been handed on to him, and she took Fleur with her into that marble palace where neither had been before. They sat in the grand tier among hundreds of strangers in rustling clothes appropriate for the occasion. Everyone must have known beforehand what the music was to mean to them or they would not have packed themselves in so tightly, on so many levels, all the way up to the ornate ceiling. While everyone else basked in the tumultuous river of sound, Fleur seemed drowned by it, so much more defeated by the uncountable number of instruments than she'd ever been by the one violin in her own timid hands. The music was so meaningful yet without any clues, except for a single clue once in a while, one instrument alone trying to tell them something that everyone else already knew.

"We'll go soon as we can," Delia whispered, close to Fleur's ear.

When they lay down that night, Fleur asked, "The man who gave you those tickets, who is he?"

How do you say to a woman who has never had a lover, *He was my lover*? How do you say, *He's my friend* to a woman who had no friends?

Delia waited to answer until she had switched off the lamp. Then she said, "Do you remember Virginia, the day she brought her boyfriend for you to see? She came all the way to where we'd moved, and you put on your coat and walked out on them. You didn't come back until they were gone."

Over there in the dark, Fleur's reflective voice of remorse. "Did I do that? Did I really do that? I'm sorry if I hurt her feelings." The mortal pain of envy lay buried under the years.

After a while Fleur said, "You remember that job I had? That one in the dime store?"

"I used to go in after school," Delia said, "and you'd slip me a chocolate. I was so proud I had a sister who worked there."

"A man used to pick me out," said Fleur. "There were three girls but he'd always ask me to wait on him. When I think about him now, he must've been what I am now, near forty, and I thought he was old. I mean I was frightened, he was so handsome. One day he wanted to walk partway home with me. I couldn't say he couldn't do that, so I walked in the wrong direction, a long way, with you and Mama waiting for me to come home. You know what I told him? I told him our mother was beautiful and our father was dead, and I said she liked to go out. Why did I say that about poor Mama?"

Fleur, who seldom spoke, whose thoughts were so concealed that people figured she had none, told her lie about their mother to entice that stranger away from herself, down a wrong path away from Fleur, crazily struggling with desire, one evening years ago.

"After you left," said Fleur, "she never wanted me to even go to the store, but I had to go and I tried to be back as soon as I could. Once a man in a car drove up alongside me as I was coming home. He asked me to go for a ride with him. It was summer, I had on a little sleeveless blouse, and I wanted to go. I wanted to know. Mama was afraid of what could happen to me and she'd be left alone. When you were with us, when we both had jobs and took care of her when we got home, and locked the door at night and put a chair up against the knob, she wasn't so afraid. But when you left, she said we just had each other. She said you'd forsaken us."

"I didn't forsake you," said Delia. "I came back when I was between jobs and that was often because all I could find were temporary jobs. When I came up here I was sure I was going to be punished for leaving you and Mama. I was afraid there was going to be an earthquake just to punish me, and buildings would fall on me, and you wouldn't have anybody to rescue you when Mama died. I wanted to stay alive to rescue you."

Fleur had already turned toward the wall. If she forgave anyone in her life, she was so quiet about it you never knew.

Fleur came to the city in old clothes. Some things were patched in many places. She had spent her evenings over meticulous little stitches, years of stitching that women didn't do anymore but that Fleur did, living in a remote place in time, kept back in the century before she was born.

With new clothes on, with a haircut, with lipstick on, Fleur went out to look for work. She never criticized the persons who turned her away. She accepted their indifference to her, their effacing of her, their edict that there was no place in the world where she was needed. She ate hardly anything, because, she explained, she wasn't earning anything. Delia offered delicacies she had never bought for herself.

"Mama told me something," Fleur said one night, a voice from out of those isolating, effacing years. "I don't know why she didn't tell you. Unless because you went away. She said Sophie had a baby."

Delia sat up to hear. The world was opening wider than it had ever opened before, and closer than ever in that widening world was her sister Fleur and Fleur's voice.

"She said that baby was Papa. She said the man who was his father was a married man, she said he was a doctor. She said when he was dying he begged to see Sophie again, but they wouldn't let her go to him. That's all I know and I don't want to talk about it anymore."

Nothing more was needed to fuel Delia's imagination. At the turn of the century, a doctor's waiting room in a prospering city, atop silver mines, must have had a long leather divan, rugs, heavy curtains that he closed across the windows, shutting out the late afternoon light. Sophie never came to him at night. He'd be home with his wife, and she, chaste young woman, home with her parents and her brothers. Delia, entranced in her bed, slipped Sophie again and again into her lover's embrace. No brief embrace, no cruel embrace, and not just one embrace. Long embraces, while the century turned them over and over together.

Out on familiar streets, Delia saw strangers of every age who could be related to her, no matter how distantly, because anyone might be related some way to the unknown man. She knew she was exaggerating that possibility, but the world was wider, and she could imagine whatever she wished.

One night Delia asked just one question,

saying she wouldn't ask any more. "Did Mama tell you what became of Sophie?"

"I guess she died," said Fleur.

Delia could imagine Sophie, if Fleur could not and did not want to. A captive Sophie, raging along the dim hallways of that three-story house, deprived of her son though he was there, at table with her, or anywhere in the house. Did she never go out into the street with him, holding his hand, setting his cap aright, pointing out this and that, her voice light and lyrical with the pleasure of his company? Was she carried away to an asylum or did she take her own young life?

Delia took a closer look at furtive old women, alone in cafés, their gaze kept down on their pastries. Clothes like Fleur wore when she came to live with Delia, faded and mended. Sophie might have become one of those old women. Nobody knew what pleasures life had stolen from them or what pleasures they'd stolen from life, if any. Delia was afraid that Fleur and herself would grow old that way, each alone in a little café, or alone together at a table in a corner, Fleur more alone than herself because Fleur was the loneliest person in the world.

One evening on her way home, passing under an open window close above her head, Delia heard a woman singing. The music was from a radio, and the woman's soaring, silvery voice brought back her mother's laughter when their father swept her off her feet and carried her around in his strong, muscular arms. Then she felt a wave of love for them that she had not felt so overwhelmingly when they were alive. She listened until the song came to an end, not caring if the person inside the house were to look out and find her there, under the window, like a beggar or a thief.

"I heard a woman singing," said Delia that night. "It was so beautiful it made me cry."

"That last night I was alone with Mama," Fleur said, "I was sitting by her bed, waiting for them to come and take her to the hospital, and I was singing quietly to myself. She asked me, 'Why are you singing?'"

"What did you tell her?"

"I said I didn't know I was singing."

Never had Delia heard Fleur sing. Nobody else had ever heard Fleur sing. Only their mother had once heard Fleur sing.

# WORKS OF THE IMAGINATION

The silent train ascended through forest and alongside a torrent so cold and so swift the water was white, and small white birds flew up like spray. On a bridge undergoing repairs the train came to a halt. Just outside Thomas Lang's window, a workman in a black knit cap was hammering at a railing, and the silence all around isolated each ring of the hammer.

Lang arrived in Grindelwald in the evening, coming from Bern where, contrary to his intention to call on a friend from the

States and tell him about the insoluble task his memoirs had become, he had stayed only half a day and called on no one. In the early night he wandered along a path on the outskirts of the town. The day was a national holiday, and fireworks opened in languid sprays all around in the dusk, and the boom of fireworks echoed against the mountains. Someone approached him on the path, a figure twice as tall as himself. Closer, he saw it was a little girl, half as tall as himself, carrying a long stick covered with tallow, the torch at its tip casting around her a high, black figure of shadows. Up on the dark mountains small lights burned here and there, far, far apart—fires perched on the night itself. In the morning, a snowy mountain stood just outside his hotel window, brought closer by the sun almost to within reach of his hand.

On a small, quiet train he went higher,

up to Kleine Scheidegg, up to an old hotel where twelve years ago he had stayed a few days in winter, and not alone. The mountains had impressed him then as a phenomenon on display, but now he was shocked by their immensity, hypnotized by their beauty and crystal silence. Cowbells and voices rang in the silence with an entrancingly pure pitch, and the density of the stone was silence in another guise.

The elderly, elegant manager registered him at the desk in the small lobby. A very tall, strong man, also elderly, in a dark green apron, whom Lang had observed carrying up four suitcases at a time, carried up his two, while another assistant, also in a green apron, a slight, dark man, surely Spanish, graciously shy, stepped in a lively way to the foot of the wide, curving staircase and gestured for him to go up. Lang climbed the stairs with his hand on the rail.

He had not often assisted himself that way and had no need to now. He was an erect, lean, and healthy sixty, and why, then, was his hand on the banister?

The silence in the room was like an invasion, a possession by the great silent mountains. The cloth on the walls, a print of pastoral scenes with amorous couples, flute players, and lambs, roused a memory of another room, somewhere else in this hotel, where he had lain in an embrace with a woman who, at the time, was very dear. All that he remembered of the previous visit were the three persons he had been traveling with—the woman, a close friend, and the friend's wife—all now no longer in touch with him and perhaps not with one another. They had come to watch a movie being made of a novel of his. In the novel there had been only a brief mention of the Alps, but the movie director and the scriptwriter had worked out a counterfeit scene from that remark, and he had watched, amused and apart.

Once in the night he was wakened by his heart. His heart always wakened him in time for him to witness his own dying, and he waited now with his hand over his chest. When the fear subsided he took his notebook from the bedside table and fumbled to uncap his pen. Through the translucent curtains the sky and the white mountains gave him enough light to write by, but his hand was given no reason to write. Was this another place he would leave, his notebook empty? Traveling all spring and into the summer, he had found no place where he could begin his memoirs. If one place had been so full of the sound of the ocean—not just the waves, whose monotonous beat often went unheard, but the threat in the depths—another place was too full of the sounds of the city—insane noises. And in quiet places he heard, in memory, the voices of his healers back in the States, men who had never truly known just what it was he had lost, and gave the loss such facile names—confidence, faith, whatever—and the names of several persons who had been dear to him and were lost to him. These healers had promised him his completed memoirs, and other novels in the future, if only he would begin, because, they said, work itself wrought miracles and brought the spirit back from the grave. But there was a loss beyond their probing, a loss they were unwilling to accept as the finality he knew it was, a loss, a failing, that might even be commonplace and yet was a sacrilege. It was indifference, like a drugged sleep, to everyone else on earth. Ah, how could that change have come about in himself when his very reason for writing had been the belief that all life was miraculous?

He got up and drew aside the mistlike curtains. The train station was faintly lit, the awning rippling a little in the night wind. Out on the dark hills a few hazy lights burned through the night, miles apart. And beyond and all around, the luminous mountains. When he was inside the hotel their unseen presence warned him of his breath's impending abeyance, but now, gazing out at them, he felt his chest deepen to take in their cold breath across the distance, a vast breath as necessary to him as his own.

The day brought hikers up from the cities, way below. They came up in the small, silent trains, and wore big boots, thick socks, and knapsacks, as if bound for a climb of several days. But they roamed over the grassy hills for an hour or so and converged at the tables below the hotel's lower windows. They sat under colored umbrellas and under the windows' reflections of the mountains, and ate what appeared to be savory food. He kept a distance from them. There was room enough.

The only guests in the spacious parlor were far off, a family group playing cards at a table covered with green cloth. On the parquetry floors lay rich, red Persian rugs, and the many couches and chairs of antique beauty took up only small space in the large room. A long and narrow glassed-in sun porch with an abundance of wicker chairs adjoined the parlor, and he paced along its length, remembering the hotel in winter, the parlor's black-and-white marble fireplace ablaze, the pleasurable jostling and agitation of the many guests, and the hieroglyphs of distant, dark figures against the snow. He settled himself at a large table in a corner of the parlor, but all he could do was trace the glow and grain of the wood around his empty notebook.

On his way down the hall, restless, wondering if he would move on the next day, he paused before the first of several framed photographs along the wall, an early one of four climbers assembled in the photographer's studio against a backdrop of a painted mountain, all in hats and ties and heavy boots, with pots, picks, a goat. Few attempted the scaling of mountains in those years; now climbers were swarming up every mountain on earth. Farther along, he stopped before a photograph of *Der Eiger*, the mountain looming up over this hotel and over the town, miles below, a sheer, vertical face of stone. White lines were painted on the photograph, marking the ascents to the top, and at the base were the names of the fallen, preceded by white crosses. He passed along before the faces of the triumphant ones, a row of them, all young, and spent a longer time before a couple from Germany, a man and a woman, she a strongly smiling blonde and he a curly-haired handsome fellow, the kind who would take a woman along.

Then he went out, keeping apart from the many hikers who walked in a line toward Eiger as if on a pilgrimage. He strode over the lush grass, over the rise and fall of the hills, and on the crest of a hill he halted to take a look at the great stone's face. Two figures were slowly, slowly, climbing. His vision lost them in an instant and it took him some time to locate them again, so small were they and at the mercy of the atmosphere, appearing and disappearing. He sat down on the grass to watch them, his hand above his eyes to prevent the sun from playing tricks on him. The roar of an avalanche shocked him, convincing him that a mountain was collapsing, and then he saw the source of the thunder—a small fall of snow, far, far away. Somewhere he had read that the Alps had moved one hundred miles from their original location in Italy, and he wondered if the move had been centuries long, or cataclysmic, in a time when there were no human beings around to be obliterated. When his eyes began to ache from the searching, from the finding and losing of the specks that were his climbers, he returned to his room and lay down, his hand over his stone-struck eyes.

Toward twilight, when no one sat under the mountains' reflections, when they had all gone down on the trains, he went out again, strolling to higher ground over patches of tiny wildflowers that were like luminous rugs on the grass. Up near the entrance to the train tunnel that cut through stone to the top of the Jungfrau, he came to a large, heavy-wire pen where several restless dogs roved. The dogs resembled wolves, tawny with black markings, and their wild intelligent Mongol faces reminded him of the faces of nineteenth-century Russian writers. It was a comparison that amused him, and he felt light-headed over it. They paused to look into his face and into his eyes, slipped by along the fence, then returned, curious about him as he was about them. Soon in the darkening air he felt he was gazing at Gogol, at Tolstoy, at Chekhov, their faces intent on his own.

Stumbling a time or two, he made his way back down to the hotel that stood in a nimbus of its own lights. Before he went in he took a last look at the great stone. No fire burned anywhere on its enormous expanse. The climbers had made a bivouac for the night on a ledge and were already asleep. Late in the night he was wakened by a deep wondering about the couple on the ledge. The fact of their lying on a ledge somewhere on that great stone stirred in him a concern for all persons he had ever loved. Then he slept again, and the couple was lying somewhere on the cold vastness of the night, on no ledge.

In the morning he went out under an overcast sky, before any hikers appeared. The stone was monstrous. Each sight of it failed to diminish, by repetition, the shock of it. So steep was the north side, the mountain must have been split down the very center, and the other half was a hundred miles away. The climbers were not yet halfway up the wall. Often, as before, he lost sight of them, found one again and not the other, and then found the other after losing the first. After a time he covered his eyes to rest them. If they fell, would the silence and the distance deny to him the tragicness of their end? He lowered his hand, searched again, and found one dark figure on a snowy ledge. The figure fell the instant he found it. It fell so fast he was unable to trace its fall and unable to find it on a lower ledge or at the base. Nowhere, now, was the other climber. Then both had fallen, and their mortal terror struck at his heart. With his hand on his chest he went back over the hills to the hotel.

No one was at the desk in the lobby, neither the manager nor one or the other of his assistants in their green aprons. One of them would confirm the tragedy. Somewhere, back in an office, there must be a radio voice informing everyone of the climbers' fate. Outside, the murmur of the crowd under the umbrellas and the fitful, labored music of an accordion were like the sounds the deaf make, that are unheard by them. In the parlor he found the shy assistant passing through, the one he was convinced had been a child refugee from the Spanish Civil War.

"*El hombre y la mujer en la montaña, ellos se cayeron?*"

The man smiled sadly, graciously, implying with his smile that if he did not understand Spanish at least he understood the importance of the question for the one who asked it.

With faltering German he tried to repeat the question, but a strong resistance, following disappointment, whisked away his small vocabulary. He went back to the lobby.

The manager, wearing a fine suit the same gray as his hair, was now standing at the desk, glancing through some papers. A fire wavered in the small fireplace.

"The couple on Eiger, they fell?"

The manager's brow, high, smooth for

a man his age, underwent a brief overcast. "May I ask who?"

"The couple on Eiger."

"Ah, yes, the photographs in the corridor? Only those who succeeded. Only those."

"The couple up there now," he said.

"There is no one climbing now."

"Then they fell?"

"No one is climbing and no one is falling."

Lang went up the stairs, hand on the rail, a weakness in his being from the lives lost, no matter if the climbers were only specks, motes, undulations of the atmosphere. Up in his room he sat down at the desk, opened his notebook, and wrote the first word on the first of the faint lines that he likened now to infinitely fine, blue veins.

# WOMEN IN THEIR BEDS

*Dr. Zhivago . . .*

      Over the hospital's paging system the three pranksters sent their solemnly urgent voices along the corridors and into the wards, imbuing each name with a reverential depth.

*Dr. Jekyll . . .*

They were actors and playwrights, these three, Angela and Dan and Lew, social workers only temporary, offering their wit as a lightening agent to the dread air in this formidable row of faded-brick buildings,

grime the mortar. Out of place, this row—
it belonged in another part of the country,
more north, more east, under slanting rain
in Seattle or slashed by cold winds in Chi-
cago or on that penal island off New York,
someplace where the weathers punish the
inmates even more.

Yet here it was, in San Francisco's
warmest neighborhood and only a short
walk from the broad grassy slopes and
flourishing trees of Dolores Park where,
on Sundays in summer, their troupe, their
quick-change dozen actors, set up their
shaky stage and satirized the times with
their outrageous comedies, their own
commedia dell'arte, come alive again now
in the sixties. Their high-flung voices,
along with the noises they made that
thumped and banged on the neighborhood
doors, might even have reached the hospital's murky windows, sounding within like

the mutterings inside the head of the patient in the next bed.

Dan held a master's in political science and Lew a bachelor of arts in drama, but Angela, a small-time, odd-job actress, bold on stage but not as herself, had no degree whatsoever.

"Say you do," Dan insisted. "Give yourself an M.S. in sociology and a B.A. in psychology. Imagine you're speaking the truth. You do it all the time on stage."

"I don't know how long I'll last," she said.

"Nobody knows that," said Lew. "They're all wondering the same thing in there."

"I mean I may not last more than a couple of days."

Angela Anson, her name in a plastic badge on her blouse, confidante without credentials, passed up and down the women's ward, telling those on her list where they'd be going, what haven with its ominously pretty name or the bed that was waiting at home, whether longed for or not.

Unlike the men's ward where, she was told, men cursed and struck the air and straggled out into the halls on their thwarted way home, this women's ward was a quiet one. Three long rows of beds, one row along each long wall and one row along the back and, on overcrowded days, another row down the center. Narrow beds with rails that went up and down, white sheets sliding on rods for each woman's very own curtains when the doctors came by. Earthquake-prone, each morning the women's ward appeared to have undergone a quake in the night. The row of beds down the center gone, or the back row gone, and the shocked atmosphere like that after a quake. *What's happening here?* The question on each face upon a pillow. A quake of the mind, a quake of the heart.

*Dr. Curie . . .* Dan's good morning to Angela.

"Bad dreams at night," she'd told him. "My mother berating me for what? It must be because I never knew enough about her. She may have wanted to unfold herself for me and never could. Their lives must be unfolding before their eyes, in there, and they're unfolding mine. They're unfolding me. Do you know what I mean?"

Dan said he sort of knew. So she was . . . *Dr. Curie . . .* discoverer of so much that was undetectable and that might not even exist.

Her step, always a light step, was even lighter here, a step for museums and churches, sanctified places that always made her feel unworthy. *The county hospital is not a holy place, Dan said, and you were*

*not hired for the role of St. Teresa of Avila.*
*She kissed the lepers' lesions and that's not*
*in your line of duty.* Her step was light for
another reason. She wished to disappear
from this unfolding scene as the women did,
overnight, two, three, or an entire row at
a time, gone to places called home or gone
for reasons unknown to her, and as the interns also disappeared and were replaced by
look-alikes.

The illustrious doctors, long dead or
never alive, whom Dan and Lew were calling for, seemed more solidly in person than
these young interns who stepped from bed
to narrow bed, graceless, at a loss, not yet
adept in the presence of women in their
beds, maybe any woman in any bed, anywhere. Dan called these interns by their first
names, drank coffee with them, gave them
his dissident view of Vietnam, and, more
often than not, he was the one calling for

the imaginary doctors, convinced they'd be around long after the real ones, the sleep-deprived, baffled fledglings, were gone a thousand times over.

An Audience of One who never blinked. They had to imagine that God was watching, or that's what Angela had to imagine for them, these women in this pale ward, so they'd not be overlooked. So many persons in rows—it was a common enough sight across the world in Vietnam, on the television screens that seemed invented for just that repetition of wars and disasters that laid people out in rows. Over the other scenes there was always a terrible struggle in the air, but in this women's ward there was a yielding to whoever was watching over them and to the medication that must seem like a persuasive stranger entering their most intimate being for their own good. What an unbearably rude intrusion, then—Angela appearing at bedside to tell them where they'd be going next.

"Where?"

This one, this woman, fifty, pink-champagne hair, must have run away from home at nine and kept on running away. The nights of her life on a barstool till 2:00 a.m. and the last hours of the morning with a newfound friend, down in the dubious comfort of his bed. A chic hat and a string of pearls and a job, all that to begin, and then the nylons bagging at the knees and ankles and the high heels bending inward.

"Where?"

"Laguna Honda." And Angela saw this woman's face draw up from her frightened heart a small girl's look of daring to flee.

Laguna Honda. Like a monastery, like a huge echoing nunnery on a hill, it belonged in Spain in the Middle Ages. With a tower, and within the tower a dimlit archway, the only light above the thick black trees whenever Angela drove past at night. She drove fast around the curve to escape her imagining of pale faces floating on deep black waters.

"You can't do that. My daughter won't let you."

Every day this mother promised the appearance of the daughter, but the daughter wasn't showing up yet. Wasn't it glib to say that the daughter was abandoning the mother because the mother had abandoned the child? A child belongs to the world—that was Angela's explanation. But if this woman was *her* mother she'd come and stand at this bedside just as she was doing now and just as she'd appeared by her mother's bed in another ward in another city. *Your heart sinks down with your mother's, Angela said to the daughter who wasn't there. Your heart sinks down and leaves your breast and may never come back. But when you're out in the street again it comes racing back, burst-ing with grief.*

Angela said, "My supervisor is still hop-ing a bed will turn up somewhere else." Oh, God, did she say *turn up*? There was no way of saying it to ease the fear of the next bed. "More where you'd like."

"No bed in this goddamn world is where I'd like."

Later that day Angela caught sight of her in a curtained-off section, her face shocked by what her limbs were doing with-out her consent, trying to run away with her as she'd run away before, over and over. *Withdrawal from alcohol, Lew explained. It never leaves the body without a terrible lovers' quarrel.*

*Dr. Faustus . . . Dr. Faustus . . .*

At her back now, the woman to whom she listened evasively sideways, head bowed, unable to come face to face.

"I beg you."

Nod, Angela, nod, and listen with one ear.

"I beg you, please ask the doctor to let me go home."

That voice, a trembling thread trying to get itself through the eye of a needle. Angela had heard it before, years ago.

"I'll ask again."

That arrogant doctor, that one with the impatiently jiggling knee, the disposing gaze—he was the one Angela had asked. Why had she picked him? To humanize him, when she ought to turn her full gaze upon this pleading woman and humanize herself.

She did. She looked into the woman's eyes and came face to face with her own Aunt Ida. That's who this woman was, after twenty years, up from that bed in the Home for those who were never to leave. Way back on the stage of her childhood, there was Aunt Ida in bed, white hair boy's cut, the thinnest wrists, the scarcest voice, the largest, darkest eyes, and there was Angela's mother in the visitor's chair, smartly clad even though the cloche hat and Cuban heels were already ten years worn, and there was Angela, five years old, plaid skirt, black patent-leather pumps, born entertainer, reciting the tale of that terrible battle between Ivan Skvinsky Skzar and Abdul Abulbul Amir, the threats, the oaths, the blows. There was little Angela at bedside, unable to believe what her mother had told her, that Ida had been the most beautiful of the five sisters, and here was Angela now, unable to believe that this woman at her elbow had ever been other than who she was now, had ever been young, a girl, twelve, sixteen, eighteen, in that flowering time.

From her very first hours in the ward

she had tried to picture them when they were young, wanting to come to their rescue by reviving them as girls again. *Oh, such lovely girls!* Wanting to do for them what she hadn't done for her Aunt Ida.

"I try to imagine them when they were girls, but I can't," she told the head nurse, Nancy, and the nurse, already verging into that same anonymity of aging, turned her head for Angela to see her deliberately uncomprehending face. "Why would you ever think to do that anyway?"

*Dr. Mabuse* . . . Dan's voice.

*Dr. Mabuse*, that decadent doctor, dispenser of opium, was calling her to join him for a coffee break in the cafeteria.

"Were you ever in Pere Lachaise cemetery?" she asked him.

"You mean have I risen?"

Dan, so healthy, his cheeks childishly rosy, his hair darkly shiny, the kindest heart, the hardest head, wrote a crackling political column for an underground weekly.

"My year in Paris, my Marceau mime time, I wandered around in there," she said.

"Gravely there?"

"Colette's monument resembles a bed."

"Nights, does she romp around on it?"

"Afternoons, too," she said. "Maybe beds are where women belong. Half the women in the world are right now in bed, theirs or somebody else's, whether it's night or day, whether they want to be or not. That's where the blame lies for some infamous messes. Take that bed of Hamlet's mother, for example, or Desdemona's, because that's where Iago saw her in his fired-up imagination, a high-born slut, sleeping with a black-amoor. I could go on and on. You persuaded me to ask for a job in this place and now you can listen to the consequences. Now I see women as inseparable from their beds."

"Bedded down in eternity?"

"Could you see that goes on my tombstone? On second thought, I don't want a stone over me. I never want to be confined. So just wrap me in my cloth coat, forget the ermine, and leave me out on some high mountain."

*Dr. Freud . . .* please . . .

Overnight, a girl lying in the narrow bed made narrower just by youth's full size and restlessness. Dark, tumbled curls, a broad face, paled and alarmed by the pumping out of that handful of pills from where they'd settled in for a long night. Off to the psych ward at the end of the day, she was no concern of Angela's.

"Please, Miss," as Angela walked by. "I'm not allowed to go to the lavatory and the nurse won't come."

Angela handed up the bedpan, defying whatever rule there might be that forbade a social worker this act of mercy. Struggling out from under the covers, the girl sat awkwardly down on the pan, atop the bed, large, long legs bared and bent.

"Lie down, lie down," Angela urged. "You do it lying down. Under the covers." And the girl went awkwardly under, probably awkward at all of life's necessary acts, suicide among them.

Angela put the bedpan under the bed and stayed on, wanting to ask outright: *Why did you want to die?* Knowing there was no answer that could be brought to the surface by a stranger at bedside or even by a social worker with honest credentials who'd ask the same question in cleverly curative ways. Angela Anson had had no simple answer, either, and wasn't asked, because nobody knew about her attempt. A skinny sixteen, awkward at everything and even at how to hope, she was saved by that very awkwardness, and she wanted to say to this girl: *After that bungled act I left my awkwardness behind, and now I remember it sort of fondly, like I would a crazy childhood girlfriend.*

*Dr. Freud . . .* Lew telling Angela that the hour was near for a visit to the psychiatric ward. She'd asked him about it. Could she peek in for a minute to see where that girl was going?

Somewhere in another of the grim buildings she slipped into the entry of that ward. The very small entry, the only place allowed her, had space enough for the Judge, a large, high-chested fellow in a finely tailored suit, the three men in gray-drab, depleted by fear of their own minds' doings and trying not to slump, and barely enough for herself.

The Judge's voice was cleaving its way through the soiled air, asking legalese questions and informing each of his destination, which asylum, what refuge. Like a scene in any number of plays, where an assassin or a priest comes to tell the prisoner what his future looks like, this was a scene in a debtors' prison for those who couldn't pay back all that civilizing invested in them. She'd been in even closer proximity to this Judge. A wedding reception at the Stanford Court Hotel atop Nob Hill, where she'd carried trays loaded with prawns and oysters up to that buttoned-up belly.

Over in a few minutes, this orderly dispersal of the deranged. The Judge left and she followed at a discreet distance, noting his brisk sort of shuffle, a slight uncertainty of step that came from sitting in judgment for so many years. If she were ever to play a high-court judge on the stage in the park, she'd stuff a bed pillow vertically down her front and take those small steps, the

uncertainty in the head repressed all the
way down to the feet.

*Dr. Caligari . . .*

Only an illusion, that this woman was
a dwarf. Recovered now, she was going
home this hour, and all Angela had to do
was walk along beside her in that enforced
wheelchair ride to the exit and beside the
slouchy orderly doing the pushing. Angela
thought *dwarf* because of her theatrical ten-
dency to recognize types from bygone centuries, and dwarfs seemed of a time of mass
deprivation. This woman in the wheelchair,
her gray hair stubble-cut, was deprived. A
cleaning woman, she'd fainted on the job—
pneumonia—and they'd had to bring her
son along since there was no one else to take
care of him while his mother was away. So
many hiding places in the city, you never
could know what went on in them until

someone was brought out and then maybe went back in again.

Hop-skipping down the corridor toward them, impeding their progress, a young doctor, an intense one, hair askew.

"Let me see your hands."

Angela's hands began to rise, palms forward. Was there some new scan that doctors had, a scientific palmistry for detecting liars and impostors and actors?

The young hyperactive doctor was bending toward the woman in the wheelchair, whose hands lay humbly in her lap, blunt hands, curved to the shape of mop handles, vacuum cleaner handles. She uncurled them under his scrutiny.

"Can you tell me," he asked, "why your son has six fingers?"

The woman's eyes were shifting along at floor level.

"My mother cursed us."

"Who?" Wobbling off his track.

"They cursed us."

Dazedly stepping aside, the young doctor allowed them to proceed down the corridor, the orderly pushing, Angela guiding.

At the side portal they waited for the son to be brought from the adjacent building and for another social worker who was to convey mother and son back to their rooms. Out from the other building and down the path, the son was being swiftly borne toward his mother, the orderly mockingly happy to be pushing the wheelchair of this mute density of a man with two fingers too many. A rough spot on the pavement and off he flies, this son, onto the lawn where he lies docile, waiting to be lifted.

*Dr. Caligari . . . please . . .*

Lew, responding to her call, showed up in the women's ward and escorted her out into the air, around a corner where she'd never been. Lew, whose long face knew everything before it was told him, listened to her anyway.

"Doctors don't know what they're getting into when they get to be doctors," she told him. "How could *she* know why her son's got that extra little finger alongside his proper one? One finger too many, or two too many, it's just a clue to what goes on in the dark where your life gets twisted into the weirdest shape before you're even born. Suppose he came into the women's ward and asked them why they're in there. They'd say, like, Oh, sure, Doctor, my old man beat me up, or my lung collapsed, or I was hit by a trolley. They'd see he was simpleminded and they'd answer him like that, because how can you say to a doctor, My karma hurts me?"

"Lower your voice."

"I don't care who hears."

"Never take a deep breath in there," he cautioned. "Take it every morning before you go in. You've lasted how many days? Six already? But be warned."

Lower your voice, take no deep breaths, step softly, and you'll be fine. When she caught the old Gypsy woman watching her, Angela flashed an impersonal smile as proof that she knew what she was doing in that ward. The Gypsy woman was sitting up in bed after three days under covers and her own matriarchal bed was awaiting her return. A Gypsy queen, ninety-six years old. Over her bony face a blending of gold leaf and copper, her sea-green eyes sunken under mole-brown lids. Around her head a kerchief, blue and red. No resemblance to the Gypsies who went up and down the train in Spain, the tiny mother and her daughter who might have been sixteen or six, begging their way. This one must have eaten very well, this one must have wrung the necks of hundreds of fat chickens and pulled out big handfuls of feathers. Fear wasn't her bedmate here, Faith was and probably had always been, keeping her heart beating for so long.

Shrewdly, she was gazing at Angela as at someone who could be ensnared by flattery. After a while she beckoned.

"Give me your hand."

On your way back into life, do you fit yourself into who you were always expected to be, for a safe return? The very thin, limp hand, covered with brown patches like islands on an old sepia chart, turned over Angela's hand, and Angela's palm lay open to the future like a part of herself that hadn't been attended to as it ought to have been, considering its potential.

"A long life."

That index finger, its knuckle like an

ancient tarnished coin, traced a line so slowly it seemed a very long way, pausing where that high road was joined or crossed by low roads, by roads not taken, and by roads down which hitchhikers came to thumb a ride. Not until she'd stepped into this ward had she begun to trouble herself over the span of her life, and now she was being told what she didn't want to know after all.

"You are a wayward girl?"

Wayward? That word wasn't around anymore. It belonged to old-time bawdy music hall skits. If she was wayward, it must be evident enough without her palm revealing it. Unlike the nurses, so trim, so starched and white, combed and capped, Angela was artfully indifferent, her dark hair untamable, her fingernails clean but their polish chipped, her blouse clean and ironed but with one button sewn back on with an unmatching thread, black kohl all around her eyes, a cheap ring from Chinatown on one finger and an even cheaper ring from a street fair on a little finger. Anyone could spot her for a working hippie, a counterculture actress, a wayward girl.

"I'm an actress," smiling like one.

Mockery now in the glintless eyes. Was mockery, too, a life-renewing pleasure? "Actresses like jewels? Yes? Yes, I know, yes. Tomorrow my children will bring my jewels for you." The mockery grasping back that gift of a long life, the giving and the taking away all in one breath.

Under the covers again the next morning, the Gypsy woman was identified only by the colored kerchief. Out of the corner of her eye Angela saw this flattening down and felt some shameful relief from that gaze. Kept most of the day at her desk in the row of social workers' cubicles, she did not come up to the ward until late afternoon.

Oh, God, what a handsome lot they were, that woman's children. Or grandchildren. Seven of them, gathered at the bed. Visitors—friends, pastors, relatives, nuns—came around in the evening hours, but here was this Gypsy family in the afternoon. Unreal, their garments biblically splendid as that coat of many colors, and all with golden skin. They were her children of whatever generation, and all to live as long as the mother.

The bed was empty.

"Candles. Can you bring candles?" a daughter asked, and a son said, "Please. Candles," a singer's sorrowing voice.

Candles? She went in search. None in the nurses' station. No candles in the desk of the social worker on vacation, now known as Angela's desk. Drawers she hadn't opened before held only a coffee mug, a quicky-glance mirror, breath sweeteners, postcards, and in the larger, bottom drawer, a pair of high-heeled pumps to wear on dinner dates. Only two of the bona fide social workers were still at their desks, and they shook their heads. No candles, and they asked no reason for candles. Maybe the lights had gone out in the lavatory.

A cubbyhole grocery store was near, a few minutes' walk away. No candles there. Sold out. Candles were a necessity in every friend's apartment. Round as oranges, long as tapers, and ordinary ones, the soft light of the flame intensifying the marijuana mood.

When she returned, empty-handed, the archangelic children were gone.

———

NIGHT IN HER own bed, the bed she was sure to remember as the one in this period of her life, lying beside her lover whose bed it was, too, she wondered if those women ever wondered about her, about where her bed was and whether she shared it and with whom. If wonder and curiosity were signs of life, she'd give them a boost back into life by telling them some things about herself while waiting for sleep.

Listen, my dear alones, over there across the city. Do you remember how each time you lay yourself down in a bed you wondered, if even for a moment, what you were doing there? And what about the beds you thought you'd chosen yourself? Do they now seem chosen for you? Destiny's hand patting them down. *Lie here, lie here.* God must surely have created beds for sharing, for most of mine were shared and see the ways you've shared yours, given your children to hold dearly close and given your mates and your lovers. And maybe that's why a bed of solitude is so sweet, so sweet, if it's only for a while and not forever. And even if it's forever, I don't know that yet. Tonight I'm lying beside a man, a friend, who is as much in need as myself of a friend to lie down with, make love with, share the rent with, share soup with, break bread with, and lie down with again. Over against the wall, his side, is a large orange acrylic nude, because he's an art student and large nudes promise largeness of future and fortune, as always. This bed, if you want to know, is sprinkled with those tiny pellets of lint that never get to form in your beds, and it's in a very small concrete apartment, a basement apartment that's next to the boiler room, if a boiler is that monster hot water tank that supplies steamy hot water to the tenants on the six floors above, and through the night that tank heats up all of a sudden, over and over, with a rush and a roar, scaring me out from under my camouflage of sleep and unheard by my bedmate. I remember that first bed ever where I lay beside a lover. It was a bed I didn't know was there, it was just a wall in a darkened apartment, and out it came and down, like a meaning unfolding in that time when so many meanings were unfolding and I was just fourteen. Oh, then there was the bed in that home for unwed mothers, the Crittenden it was called, a name like a chastising ruler, but really a kind place, a big brick building as ancient as Laguna Honda and the place where you are tonight. A man comes to sit by his mother's bed every afternoon. Have you noticed him? Fifty, but resembles a fawn, wears a suit, a tie, places his hat on his knees. A gentle man, a fine son, and the head nurse Nancy is in love with him. I won't be mortally wounded when the son I gave life to sits someday by the bed of a mother who's not me. Old mothers in their beds all look the same. Some night, some day, there'll be Angela Anson herself in your row, and what will I say to soften the heart of the social worker who I'll dislike at first sight? Why, I'll say I was an actress with a flair for comedy, even called delightful in the theater section of the Sunday papers, even called delectable, and I'll know as I tell her, if I tell her, that she won't believe a word of it. I'll say I'd thought an actress had a special kind of destiny, a beneficent role to play, bringing to life a lot of other women. Maybe, to amuse her, I'll tell her about the pranks we played, Dan and Lew and myself, calling for those doctors who were so real for us and unreal for everybody else. And if she's not amused, I'll tell her, whether it's true or not, that Dan became a high-class political columnist, syndicated, and Lew a drama professor at a prestigious university, but I won't tell her that all my stages were small ones, if that's true for me. I'll say all that, hoping in my heart, my frightened heart, that I've persuaded her not to drop me off into that black lagoon. Oh, my dears, have you ever heard these lines? *I in my bed of thistles, you in your bed of roses and feathers.* I thought it meant the other woman's bed, *her* bed of roses and feathers, where the lover I'd loved so much was lying, but now I know it means so much more and I'll tell you why. Just remember the beds where you wished you weren't and the beds where you wished you were, and then name any spot on this earth that's a bed for some woman this very hour. A bed of stones and a bed of earth trampled by soldiers and a bed of ashes, and where you're lying now,

where you never wanted to imagine your-
selves. If I'd wished for a bed of roses and
feathers, and *I did, I did*, now I don't want
it so much anymore.

A candle. The candle she'd been looking for was on the table in plain sight, an
average one, white, flickering away as candles do, showing her the plates and glasses
and paint tubes around it, the clothes on
the chair, his orange nude against the wall,
Molière's plays on the bed, the covers over
the sleeping man beside her and over herself,
not alone and yet alone. If she were to take
that candle up to the ward, a light for any
woman leaving at any time, even when she
herself wouldn't be there anymore, would
that be going too far? An actress, carried
away by her role?

DR. CURIE . . .

Once again, Dan was bidding her a

good morning. She heard his voice along the ceiling of the ward as she went up one aisle and down another, carrying the white candle in its wooden holder. In the ward's daylight its tip of flame was probably not discernible by the women at a distance, but surely they knew the candle was lit and the women who were closest to it knew.

At her back now, Nurse Nancy. "What's this all about?"

"The Gypsy woman," said Angela. "Her children asked me to bring a candle."

"That was yesterday," said Nurse Nancy, the only nurse with gray hair and whose step was flat, wearier than the other nurses' steps. "They've got their own to-do, whatever they do. They've got their own candles." Searching Angela's eyes to see if this act confirmed a strangeness within.

"I thought the women might appreciate it," said Angela.

"The other ladies don't know she's gone. They've got their own problems."

And Nurse Nancy blew out the flame, with a breath that failed to be strong and unwavering but did the job anyway.

Lightly, then, a touch at Angela's elbow and a touch at her back, touches to assist her to stay on her feet and to point her in the right direction. Or were they touches of complicity?

COUNTERPOINTS